He raised

Like he'd raised it to her during his speech to *my bride, who seems to have surprised everyone, but humbled me, by accepting my proposal*. There'd been chuckles in the crowd at that, even though Simone doubted Leo did much of anything without knowing the answer first. As for their engagement? There was no surprise about it at all.

He'd been suddenly overcome by the need to find a bride and she'd watched his frustrated efforts with a professional matchmaker, unable, it seemed, to find him the right wife. She'd seen the generous prenup drawn up for whoever this fictional bride might be. In a frustrated moment in his office he'd asked her, possibly unseriously, *Why can't I find someone like you?* Then, in a moment of desperation, Simone had uttered the fateful words. *Maybe you can...*

When **Kali Anthony** read her first romance novel at fourteen, she realized a few truths: There can never be too many happy endings, and one day she would write them herself. After marrying her own tall, dark and handsome hero in a perfect friends-to-lovers romance, Kali took the plunge and penned her first story. Writing has been a love affair ever since. If she isn't battling her cat for access to the keyboard, you can find Kali playing dress-up in vintage clothes, gardening or bushwhacking with her husband and three children in the rainforests of South East Queensland.

Books by Kali Anthony

Harlequin Presents

Revelations of His Runaway Bride
Bound as His Business-Deal Bride
Off-Limits to the Crown Prince
Snowbound in His Billion-Dollar Bed
Awoken by Revenge

Behind the Palace Doors...

The Marriage That Made Her Queen
Engaged to London's Wildest Billionaire
Crowned for the King's Secret

Royal House of Halrovia

Royal Fiancée Required
Prince She Shouldn't Crave

Visit the Author Profile page at Harlequin.com.

VOWS TO THE BOSS

KALI ANTHONY

PRESENTS

MIX
Paper | Supporting
responsible forestry
FSC® C021394
www.fsc.org

Harlequin®
PRESENTS™

PLEASE RECYCLE
THIS PRODUCT IS RECYCLABLE

Recycling programs
for this product may
not exist in your area.

ISBN-13: 978-1-335-21353-2

Vows to the Boss

Copyright © 2026 by Kali Anthony

For questions and comments about the quality of this book, please contact us at CustomerService@Harlequin.com.

TM and ® are trademarks of Harlequin Enterprises ULC.

Harlequin Enterprises ULC
22 Adelaide St. West, 41st Floor
Toronto, Ontario M5H 4E3, Canada
www.Harlequin.com

HarperCollins Publishers
Macken House, 39/40 Mayor Street Upper,
Dublin 1, D01 C9W8, Ireland
www.HarperCollins.com

Printed in Lithuania

VOWS TO THE BOSS

Naz, thank you for the conversations over our endless passion for Presents heroes, romance, these books that make us laugh and cry, and the stories which we're privileged to write. Thank you also for your advice when my characters aren't playing nicely, and helping me convince them to behave (or at least, misbehave in the best possible ways!). Here's to many more years of the magic that is writing these glorious books about love. There could be nothing more joyous than that.

CHAPTER ONE

LEO KNEW IT wasn't *who* you invited to your wedding that was important. It was those you *left off* the guest list that made your wedding an occasion to be talked about. He'd left plenty off his guest list for his wedding today. The writers of magazines and style blogs had estimated the number of guests would be in the many hundreds. They were wrong. Instead, those invited had been chosen strategically, with thought and care. Royalty mingled with commoners, select clients with trusted suppliers. Each invitation sending a message about where Leonardo Zanetti was now placed in the world, who had helped him to get there and where he wanted to be in the future. It was one of the things that made his wedding to Ms Simone Taylor the most talked about of the year.

Leo counted on the talk.

A crucial business deal relied on it. He *would* purchase the Tessitore textile company and in doing so cut the knees from Vito and Rocco Silvestri. Father and son. *His* father and his half-brother. Makers of world-renowned, bespoke furniture that was bought by princes, and coveted and poorly copied by paupers. They were the only ones who mattered to Leo and, when he had his way, they'd never use another metre of Tessitore fabric in their coveted designs, ever again.

A perfect means to avenge his mother's memory, using the father who'd stolen everything from them both. If Vito hadn't done so, Leo's mother would have still been alive.

A cold knife of guilt stabbed through him, lethal as the black ice that had stolen his mother's life all those cruel years earlier. Back then, he was an angry teenager, tired of being impoverished and living hand to mouth on his mother's meagre cleaning wage.

Instead of staying in Milan with her, he'd run to Rome to try and seek his fortune. There, he'd learned painful lessons about what poverty and hunger of the body and spirit *truly* meant.

How easy it was, when you were cold and famished in squalor on the streets and too full of pride to scuttle home with your tail between your legs, to fall in with people who made you feel you were someone else entirely. Powerful and important, when the ugly truth was, you were nothing but fodder for their illegal enterprises.

It turned out that, for a while, crime did pay. Yet not enough for the lifestyle he'd wanted to live. Leo's mother had paid the price of his failure to support her. Leaving a job one winter morning she slipped on the icy stairs. A simple fall, a mundane accident. Yet one with catastrophic consequences.

That was when life as he had known it had ended.

Since then he'd risen like a tainted phoenix from the ashes of his rage and grief.

'Everything okay?' Simone, his executive assistant and now wife, asked.

They'd been at a table mingling with guests who he considered to be some of his few allies in a world of old-money rivals. Amongst people who wanted to tear him down for the temerity of coming from nothing and making something of himself. This wedding was as much for work and shoring up alliances as it was for showing the world he'd put aside his playboy single days and 'settled down'. Still, Leo regretted that in his introspection he'd been ignoring Simone.

Whilst they both well knew the purpose of this marriage was business and not pleasure, now wasn't the time to be thinking all about himself. This was her day as much as his. More to the point, failing to focus on her wasn't a good look when they were supposed to be blissfully in love.

The mere thought churned acid in his gut. To Leo, love equalled being used, betrayed and abandoned. He'd learned that lesson well, taught by his father's neglect. Nothing he'd witnessed as an adult had convinced him differently.

'Everything's perfect,' he said. Aside from his dark thoughts that was, but Leo was sure he'd hidden them well enough. He was a master of disguise, after all. 'Why wouldn't it be?'

For good measure Leo threw out his trademark smile. The one that had earned him his first million-dollar pay check at the age of nineteen, after he'd been plucked from the Milan streets by a talent scout in the days after his mother's funeral.

He'd rocketed to the heights as a top model in a viral and now-famed aftershave commercial, which had earned him dizzying amounts of money. Then he walked away from it all and opened his style and design company, Circolo.

A role where he was feted by the rich and famous for his impeccable taste and advice on how they could achieve it for themselves. One which had made him his first billion dollars before he'd turned thirty.

The story told was an old and well-worn one. Seen as the ultimate fairytale every time the press dredged it up. But all Leo could think at the time was that his face and body were finally good for something more than picking up women or inflicting fear on Rome's small business owners.

Simone raised an arched brow and cocked her head. Her silvery gaze should have been cool and assessing. Yet the soft smokiness of her eyes and plush pout of her generous pink lips, so different from the barely-there makeup she usually wore, painted another picture entirely. Her intensity in this moment wouldn't have been out of place in their two-bedroom suite, alone, with both of them contemplating their approaching wedding night.

To hell with the separate bedrooms they'd agreed on…

A shocking heat ignited, settled in his gut, then scorched much lower. Leo schooled his face into neutrality. He was used to hiding his feelings. A skill learned in his modelling days pretending he was basking on a warm summery beach after a cooling swim, when in truth he was wet and freezing in a bitter winter's breeze.

'You have that look. Like something's on your mind,' she murmured.

There was a prickle of recognition. An uncomfortable sensation, like he was being exposed. Simone had an uncanny way of seeing right through him. It's what made her the finest executive assistant he'd ever worked with, being able to anticipate his needs before he even realised what he'd wanted himself. It was enough to give him pause. She didn't need to witness the errant and misplaced desire that suddenly seemed to have overtaken him. It was simply an adjustment period, that was all. Moving from the life of an avowed bachelor with any number of women similarly invested in fun-times-not-a-long-time, to one of a dutifully engaged and then married man, focused on one woman.

It didn't mean anything more. It never could.

'Business is on my mind.'

It wasn't exactly a lie. People believed his life had been charmed but recently, nothing had gone as planned. His efforts to atone for his youthful sins in Rome, finding the families he and the gang he'd run with had harmed, had run into some snags. Unnecessary questions were being asked when all he sought was to keep that part of his life his own, dark secret and repay what was owed to them through an impenetrable trust and charity. Then there was Tessitore, which he was intent on purchasing with single-minded focus. Especially after he'd discovered his father and half-brother were sniffing around, looking to purchase it too.

Simone placed her hand to her chest, her wedding and engagement rings sparkling in the soft candlelight.

'Always about business. On your wedding day too. Such a romantic, my husband.'

Husband. That word whispered through him. The real surprise was that if someone had told Leo a year ago that today he'd be married, he would have said they were deluded. Yet here he was, with a gold ring on his finger, sitting in the opulent ballroom of the finest hotel in New York, *The City That Never Slept.*

He flexed his hand. He'd always thought of a wedding ring as something akin to a noose, but this one sat comfortably snug, gleaming against his skin. To his relief, it was barely noticeable once Simone had slipped it on with cool yet unsteady fingers earlier in the day.

Their MC moved to the microphone. Given Leo had planned the running sheet for today to the last, obsessive detail, he knew this was the announcement of their first dance as husband and wife.

'Let me show you how romantic I can be,' he murmured.

People were listening, after all. Whilst everyone here were supporters, he still needed the talk about this wedding to be the right sort. How Leo Zanetti and Simone Taylor fit together perfectly, not that they presented as a discordant picture. It had been a whirlwind ever since their engagement only a few months before. There'd been no time to display themselves as a 'loving' couple, what with organising New York's wedding of the year, dealing with his concerns in Rome and the long hours trying to secure Tessitore.

The true illusion of their coupledom had meant to start today, and he was already failing. Their conversation seemed stilted, because people were watching and listening, and he was trying to play an unfamiliar part of the doting partner, rather than a casual lover. Leo stood and held out his hand palm up. Simone placed hers in his. Her flesh still cool, but solid and sure. No hint of a tremor now, which he took as a good sign. He led her towards the dance floor to scattered applause, as the band struck up a suitably romantic song.

Leo took Simone into his arms, trying to remember that he should hold her as if she was something precious. Then he gazed down at her as intently as he could and the pupils in her shale-grey eyes flared.

'You look beautiful,' he said. Finally, a truth he could admit. The vintage satin of her one-of-a-kind 1930's wedding gown, like warm liquid underneath his palms. Slipping over her body, slick as oil, teasing his fingertips. When he'd been sleeping rough on the streets of Rome in frigid winters, all he'd dreamt of was silk and softness. Of warm perfumed bodies that would chase away the cold, make him forget the scent of rot and rubbish in the alleyways he'd kept to. Leo pushed away the memory from that time long past. Focusing instead on Simone, because praising your bride's appearance and giving her your undivided attention was the sort of thing you *should* do on her wedding day.

'Thank you. You chose everything, after all.'

Her voice struck him, soft and low. A little more raw than normal. He'd heard her speak a thousand times and yet her tone in this moment shot right through his gut with the punch of an arrow.

From Cupid's bow, some might say.

Not him.

Cupid be damned. He'd seen what love had done to his mother. How she'd been *robbed*. First of her ideas, then of *everything* by his father who'd left them for a woman who could afford to fund him as he chased his stolen dreams. As he took Leo's mother's furniture designs and opened his own business selling her ideas as his own. As he'd cast off his old life like a worn coat and started afresh with a new, wealthier woman.

'I welcomed your involvement,' he said, as they executed a spiral turn. He reeled her back in as he continued. 'Some might even say, *encouraged* it.'

Simone's body pressed against him, even closer than before. They'd had some practice with a dance instructor to ensure they'd look seamless. In those few, short classes everything had felt stiff. Stilted. Yet something about today seemed to have transformed them both. Leo noticed for the first time how Simone fit into his arms like a puzzle piece. Her scent the citrus blossom of an Italian spring. Perhaps it was a leftover from her bouquet of the same flowers? Leo could almost close his eyes and imagine being immersed in it, so intoxicating and achingly familiar.

Instead he took a slight step back, to give them both distance.

'Welcomed? Really? Mr Zanetti giving up his famed control? I don't believe it for a second.' She laughed, yet the sound was a little sharp, tinged with cynicism. He knew that sentiment well, being one of the greatest cynics of them all.

'Surely marriage is all about compromise. My *famed control* wasn't so tight that I didn't offer you any choices.'

He'd been surprised at Simone's strange disinterest in her dress or in any of the plans for the wedding itself. She'd allowed him to have the final decision on everything, including the stylist who did her hair and makeup for the day because, in Simone's words, *that's what you do, Leo.*

'I'm sure each choice was offered through gritted teeth

with a firm view on what you saw as the right one,' she said. 'Given that, it seemed easier to allow you to win from the beginning. I prefer to pick my battles. Because as you say, marriage is about compromise.'

There it was again, that spike of sensation at the realisation Simone could read him only too well. When his engagement had been announced, the rumour mill ran riot at his 'surprising' choice of bride. There'd been talk of him marrying just about every one of the many women who had graced his arm at one time or another in the past. Whether they'd been lovers or mere acquaintances, it didn't matter. Socialites, models, movie stars. All polished and perfect when they stepped out with him in public. Never once any mention of the person who was at his side in all ways.

Simone Taylor.

As he'd explained in the inevitable media storm that followed, the woman who he'd worked with closely for two years as his executive assistant, knew him better than any living human on earth. She was, therefore, a natural and inevitable choice. Throw out talk of Simone keeping him 'grounded' and the press lapped up the story of love blossoming in the heady environment of the boardroom like stray cats to milk.

That was the story they'd presented to the world and everyone had believed it, even staff at Circolo who'd been surprisingly happy about the news. The truth was far more practical.

'You *allowed* me? Did I get anything wrong?' he asked.

Most of the time he wouldn't have cared, because he *knew* his choices were right. Even when he offered options, to give the illusion of choice to some of the few clients he still dealt with personally, they always went with his first selection. As Simone had done. Yet with her, there was a strange sensation like a fishbone stuck in his gullet, that drove him to seek her answer.

'You know perfectly well you didn't. They don't call you the Sultan of Style for nothing.'

He'd been called something else, in his youth in Rome. The Handsome Viper. Sent in to 'encourage' small business owners to pay money for protection from imagined enemies, when the true enemy was him and those he worked with. If they didn't pay up? Then others in the gang would be unleashed. In the end, his looks, size and the gang's reputation got the job done and most capitulated.

Most…

He snorted. 'The Sultan of Style's a ridiculous title.'

There was that arched rise of her brow again. That intense look that speared right through him once more. Luckily he wasn't so transparent with Simone that he couldn't hide his greatest sins. She might know a lot about him, but she didn't know it all and he'd do everything in his power to keep it that way.

'But it's good for business and the press loves it. They love you.'

Her hand moved on his shoulder, almost a clench. Some quarters of the press had been unfair and unkind when he and Simone had become engaged in their reported whirlwind romance.

Plain Jane Marries Sultan of Style!

That's what one tabloid had printed and others soon followed. Unimaginative sheep, all of them.

It wasn't that Simone didn't have style. She had one which an uncharitable commentator he would never speak to again, had unfairly termed 'Funeral Director Chic'.

Leo preferred to say she was *businesslike, with a minimalist aesthetic.* Both were descriptions they'd tried seeding to the press but hadn't caught on.

Yet it rankled, a bitter pill he railed against swallowing, especially since she'd politely refused most of his efforts to gift her designer fashion. Though she had accepted a vintage item for their engagement dinner, when he'd told her it was a thrifty choice. Still Simone didn't seem to care about her appearance at all, or want to accept the offer of his credit card to facilitate some choices of her own.

What woman wouldn't want to spend his money? Most others of his acquaintance had and he'd enjoyed sharing it around. He'd never forgotten the cold, hard life he'd come from on the streets, when a little softness might have made a difference. And whilst he didn't care what was printed about him, leaving that to his PR department, he still couldn't help wondering whether Simone wasn't so circumspect about the criticism of her.

'I meant what I said.'

'You've said lots of things.'

'About you, being beautiful.'

Whilst they didn't have *that* sort of relationship, Leo was still driven to repeat his praise. Something about her seemed to light up then, in a way he'd never seen before. Her grey eyes widening a fraction. Her gloss slicked lips, parting. She didn't seem so disinterested now. His heart rate kicked a little higher, as if a world of possibilities had begun to crack open when there were really none, aside from a continuing professional relationship.

'Soon, everyone will see what I can,' Leo said.

It was a promise, and one he'd been working assiduously towards. The exclusive rights to their wedding had been sold to a popular lifestyle magazine with all proceeds donated to charity. They'd see what Simone usually hid. What he glimpsed in this moment. The way the ivory silk of her dress caressed her gentle curves. The fabric sinuous and almost alive as she moved. Her long golden hair not restrained in her usual bun or chignon, but swept back from her face by glittering combs. Tumbling over her shoulders in thick, glossy waves like a forties movie star. Add in the perfect lighting and a world-renowned photographer, and she'd finally be recognised for who she truly was.

Simone Zanetti. His *beautiful* wife.

She looked up at him, with a whisper of pink flushing her cheeks.

'I— Thank you, Leo.'

'My pleasure, *amore mio*.' Given a few guests had been invited to join them on the dance floor he'd tried the words of affection out for size, in the perfect timbre. Loud enough for the people dancing around them to hear. Soft enough to seem intimate.

They'd had no bridal party for their wedding. No one but each other. For him, because he had no family worth inviting. For Simone, it seemed her position was the same.

He was aware of her parents, as he had been with any employee who held a position of trust and importance in his company. She had a wealthy family in California. Her father was from the ivy league. Her mother, a famed socialite. Her brother was a corporate lawyer. She also had a younger sister, who hadn't yet made her way in the world.

When Leo had suggested inviting them all to the wedding she'd refused, for her mother, father and brother at least, saying they were estranged. Her sister, who she'd admitted to him when their arrangement was settled had needed her help, remained a mystery. Something about her health. That was all Simone would say on the subject. His interest had been piqued because there might have been a similarity between them he'd been unaware of before. Although for that very reason he'd let further discussion slide. Simone was entitled to her secrets. Hell knew, he was keeping enough secrets of his own.

No one knew he was the son of Vito Silvestri. Leo would never give his father the satisfaction of acknowledging him in any way.

'*Amore mio*? Isn't that a little…unnecessary,' Simone whispered, jolting him from his thoughts about the man who'd donated his genetic material to Leo's life and nothing else.

Leo leaned forwards, his lips at her ear. What would the guests think? That they were having a tender moment? He hoped so.

'Accept the endearment,' he murmured, his cheek against hers. Simone's breath hitched and something warm and potent slid in his belly like a shot of Grappa.

'What should I call you, then?'

For so long she'd called him Mr Zanetti or Sir. When she finally used his first name, he'd liked the sound of it on her lips. Leonardo. Leo. The way she said it, as if she was savouring each syllable.

'Whatever you want.'

There was a moment of hesitation, almost a misstep in their otherwise synchronous dance.

'What about… Pumpkin?'

Dio. With that one word she could destroy his reputation overnight. Yet the question carried a smile. He could hear it in the light, playful tone of her voice. Leo wished he'd seen it on her face, since her smiles were rare and fragile things more often granted to others, such as juniors in the office who needed encouragement. Most of the time she treated him with bland professionalism.

He chuckled and she pulled back from him grinning. Her eyes twinkled under the chandeliers adorning the room. Her look of mirth burst like a firework in his chest.

He leaned forwards again. His lips now barely touched her ear. The tease of them achingly close, the desire to connect and hear her sigh in pleasure, sang through him. This was not how things were supposed to be, his reactions unfamiliar after two years of them working together in a way that was entirely businesslike.

'Let's stick with *Leo*. Though I can teach you words of love in Italian should you so wish, *cara*.'

A tremor ran through her, like a fault line suddenly cracking. What was he thinking? Simone was a woman who'd been clear about what she'd wanted from him and what she didn't. It had aligned with his views *perfectly.*

He'd rejected any idea of marrying, until his reported playboy past became an impediment to the Tessitore family, whose heritage textile company had been family owned for hundreds of years. In all the wargaming over a possible buyout, it was the only sticking point he and his marketing department could see to him purchasing it. The Tessitores' increasingly concerned comments about his stability and Circolo's plans for succession. In truth, he had none. No desire for marriage or family, unlike his *father* whose own family seemed to be a small and perfect Italian success story. Yet what nobody knew was that the immensely successful Silvestri company had been started on the back of his mother's designs. Stolen when his father had left his mother and Leo behind.

'Leo, then,' she whispered, the brush of her breath caressing his cheek.

'*Perfetto.*'

He pulled back and looked down on her again. She'd picked up some Italian in their time together and this was another word she clearly understood, as a whisper of pink flushed her high cheekbones. He couldn't explain why witnessing her awareness of him appealed, because it shouldn't have. Their relationship wasn't one built on romance. Both had agreed on that.

Passion, however, was another matter entirely. Could still waters run deep?

What would it be like to dive in and find out?

'Nothing's ever perfect, *Leo.* Not even you.'

It was a salutary reminder of her opinion of him. So many executive assistants he'd employed had been...unsettled by him in some way. Female, male, younger, older. It made no difference. Except her. After her three-month probation had ended with a permanent contract, she'd stalked into his office with a spoken demand.

Stop dazzling the staff, Mr Zanetti.

It was rather like being attacked by a tiny kitten.

He enjoyed her claws.

Although *she* never appeared dazzled or affected by him at all. She seemed wholly unfazed. But as he'd told her, it was hard not to dazzle when you regularly hit the top ten world's best-looking men lists. It wasn't that he was vain; rather, Leo was pragmatic about the realities of his situation, as he'd told her.

It comes with the territory, Ms Taylor.

After that, he'd smiled and she'd turned on her practical heels and stalked right out again.

The mood had been set between them on that day and it hadn't changed much since.

'You're poor for my ego, Simone.'

Her face might have seemed impassive, but he glimpsed a silvery spark in her eyes. He didn't know why he thought so, but he almost *heard* her wanting to roll them.

'Stop. What I say has no impact on your rudely healthy ego. None. At. All.'

Funny that was exactly the same as he'd thought of her. His words were like rain from a roof, water off a duck's back.

'Does anything I say have an impact on yours?'

She cocked her head. 'You think I have an ego?'

He didn't doubt it, given how they'd become engaged. As his executive assistant, Simone had been fully aware of his efforts to find a wife, the reasons for his sudden quest for matrimony. She'd located a world-renowned matchmaker and worked with his lawyer to ensure his wishes were documented in an appropriate pre-nuptial agreement, in anticipation of a marriage. Yet he'd been overcome by frustration at the process, how the women he'd been matched with never seemed quite right. They'd been looking for love, or at least for something *more*. They weren't interested in his work, when his work was his *life* and what drove him.

The efforts to meet someone and engage in something with the hope of it being forever had become increasingly tedious, because his whole life so far had been about the temporary. The reset to permanence was an uncomfortable one. It didn't feel right, like wearing a poorly-made suit.

In a frustrated moment, after a failed lunch date with yet another beautiful woman who didn't *fit*, he'd returned to the office, glimpsed Simone and spat out the almost careless but perhaps his most insightful words he ever said.

Why can't I find someone like you?

She'd cocked her head at him, just like she'd done tonight, fixed him with her assessing gaze and then given the fateful reply.

Maybe you can.

What had started out as something entirely fanciful, sparked an idea that sunk its teeth into him and wouldn't let go. That in a world of people who wanted things he wouldn't give, here was a woman who only sought what he could.

In the beginning his negotiations were cautious because he valued Simone more as his executive assistant than anything else. His right hand in so many ways. Yet she'd been clear, harbouring no secret desires for love.

She wanted her job, and money she couldn't raise even with her generous wage, to help her sister Holly.

Some tweaks to their pre-nuptial agreement and it was done. No need for any more dinners or painful 'getting-to-know-you' sessions, since both of them knew enough about the other to make the arrangement work.

And what they didn't know, wouldn't hurt them.

'You propositioned me, so you clearly believed you were worth it.'

The corner of her lips tilted in an enigmatic, Mona Lisa smile. Had Da Vinci ever sought to discover what was going through his subject's mind as he immortalised one of the most famous smiles in history? Because for Leo, what was going through his wife's mind had begun to intrigue him in ways he hadn't thought possible.

'You accepted, so you clearly understood I was.'

It was an enticing exchange. Their banter, such as it was when Simone was only his assistant, had always been professional. Now, with this woman in his arms, there was a whisper of something more. Yet she still regarded him with her wintry grey eyes, impassive and confounding.

'Once the seed was sown, Simone, I never had any doubt.'

A truth, in his carefully crafted life of lies.

The music began to slow, then stop. From the perfectly timed running sheet, Leo knew this was the end of the evening. He let Simone go and she moved away from him, stepping to his side. For a brief and unscripted moment he wanted to tell the band to start up again, so they could have one last dance, where he could hold her and they could continue this push and pull, and then he might find out what she truly thought of him. However, that would ruin the theatre of the evening, so he restrained himself as his guests clapped and they moved to what should have been the perfect send off. Except it wasn't perfect, when all he wished for was the impossible.

To have Simone in his arms again.

CHAPTER TWO

Simone leaned against the rich wooden wall of the lift taking them both to the suite Leo had booked for their wedding night, to save on getting stuck in traffic. Really, it had seemed unnecessary when they could have simply returned to his townhouse. Her stomach swooped uncomfortably. This unsettling feeling didn't have anything to do with spending their first night living together. That couldn't be it at all.

As Leo's executive assistant, she'd spent two years in his proximity. They'd travelled together in his jet. She'd worked long nights and stayed in his brownstone, though admittedly in a suite designed exclusively for guests. She even kept spare clothes there, just in case. Being this close to him had never affected her before.

It had to be due to the speed with which the lift moved towards the top floor of the hotel. Nothing else.

Simone shook off the strange sensation, glancing at Leo's imposing profile as he stared ahead of him, seemingly lost in thought. A few bits of coloured confetti clung to his coal-dark hair and were sprinkled on the shoulders of his impeccable tuxedo made specially for their wedding. She *knew* he owned four other tuxedos already, so he could simply have taken one from his closet and been done. Why bother with the cost of another?

But that wasn't Leo Zanetti and never would be. He liked the excess of it. The admiring comments when he was seen in something new, even if it was a suit. No doubt the magazine that would write the article about their 'whirlwind romance' and show pictures of their wedding to the world, had already been given details of their wedding attire. Especially when Leo could make or break a tailor with a raised eyebrow when someone asked him about the fit of a suit. Or create a whole design trend just by saying he liked something.

It was so…frivolous. Like her own life had been before she'd smashed the mould made for her by her parents. Still, even with all of that, the night had caught her by surprise. Setting aside the breathless members of society gushing over the wedding, something about it had seemed unusually weighty. Their vows, all traditional. Promises made to one another, even if they were meaningless and only made to be broken.

It all sat heavily on her chest, pressing down on her. Making it hard to breathe…

Probably just a hangover from the realisation that the moment represented a final nail in the coffin of her childhood dreams. Of finding her prince, falling in love and marrying. Some things were clearly ingrained in her, even though life had taught Simone years ago that love wasn't to be trusted. She'd decided then to rely on herself and no one else.

The lift eased to a stop and Leo turned to her, their gazes clashing. His eyes a shade of blue so vibrant and shocking it always caught her by surprise. Like a jump-scare, except with a frisson not entirely unpleasant, the way those eyes of his pierced her very soul.

You look beautiful.

Her breath caught. The memory of those words still slipping seductively through her.

Simone knew she wasn't beautiful in any traditional sense. Her mother had told her that, often enough. That she had an *interesting face.* Eyes a touch too narrow, mouth a little too wide. Blessed with good hair, though, to her mother's relief. She'd spent her teens and early twenties trying to live up to the impossible expectations set for her by her family in her comportment and the way she'd dressed. Wearing couture and designer brands like others wore off the rack. It had all been so meaningless. Her true thoughts on anything had been irrelevant. All that was important was meeting her parents' exacting standards. Saving herself for marriage and marrying well, which meant marrying someone her parents chose for her.

Simone hadn't sought out praise for her appearance in years. Didn't need to. She'd become tired of people trying to turn her into something *they* wanted her to be and so she'd left that life behind. She was who she was, now. So why did Leo's comment twine its way round her like gift-wrapping ribbon? Silver and sparkly. It must have been the champagne at the wedding reception, making her a little fuzzy, even though she hadn't drunk that much…

'Would you like a nightcap?' Leo asked as the doors slid open to their suite, all warm neutrals and impeccable styling. The lights of her adopted home city like a kaleidoscope beyond the floor to ceiling windows. Central

Park a dark, velvety patch, hemmed by the twinkling cityscape surrounding it.

Simone wanted to take the jewelled combs from her hair, wash off her makeup and process the day. Remove her wedding dress, the bias-cut moulding to her, draping her body like liquid embodied in fabric. She hadn't worn anything like it for years, her life more about practical-ity now than being a hated mannequin on display for her family. The heavy satin slipped seductively across her skin, so smooth and silky it almost felt like a negligee rather than a wedding dress. A mix of feelings swirled in her belly at the memories of the evening they'd just left. How Leo had held her on the dance floor as if she was in some way precious to him. How he'd looked at her as if he'd *seen* her for the first time.

'Sure,' she said. Perhaps against her better judgement, but a final drink would be a reasonable full stop to what had otherwise been a long day. She hadn't really had one like it, with all the plucking, primping and pamper-ing, since her Debutante Ball nine years earlier, when she'd been another woman altogether. 'But before we do, you have…'

She reached out and brushed his suit, scattering some of the coloured paper onto the carpet. His shoulders were broad and strong under the fine wool, as she'd known in-tellectually but discovered for real, when they'd danced for the first time. The strength in those shoulders might carry the weight of the world if you allowed them to.

Leo's eyebrows rose and she pulled back as if burned. What was she doing? She just knew Leo would hate to know that he still had confetti sprinkled on him. The man was impeccable in all things. Nothing out of place unless he'd styled it that way, or it had been styled for him.

'Any more?' he asked. His voice deep and a little rougher than usual.

There was some in his hair. For a fleeting moment she imagined brushing her hand through the strands to scatter the confetti to the floor. Simone's fingers prickled as she wondered what all that dark hair would feel like. Thick, no doubt, but soft? Wiry? No... *Impossible.*

Simone waved her hand about the general direction of his head, and his eyes widened.

'In your hair.'

He raked his fingers through his hair and the confetti fluttered to the floor, just as she imagined it would. His hair was now perfectly dishevelled in a way Leo was an expert at mastering. '*Grazie.* You're similarly afflicted.'

He didn't try to touch her and she didn't know why it stung. Simone moved to a mirror, barely recognising the woman who looked back at her like a ghost. A reflection of who she'd once been, not who she'd become. With soft, smoky eyes. Blushing pink lips. Hair gleaming and curled, tumbling over her shoulders. The hours it had taken to achieve this look.

In the reflection stood Leo, a little off to the side. His gaze on her in the mirror was intent. Though it always tended to be, his focus taking some getting used to, until you realised that it infiltrated every part of his life. From how he dressed, to how he worked, to how he exercised. Perhaps even to how he loved, if the string of women who'd constantly graced his arm on any given month was anything to go by. She wondered how it was possible for him to maintain that level of intensity. Their eyes met in the mirror. His gaze held hers with a hint of awareness.

He thought she was beautiful.

High praise, coming from a person often voted the most beautiful man on the planet.

She dismissed the moment, focusing instead on the confetti that adorned her as well. She couldn't brush her hands through her hair because that was likely impossible. A wedding hairstyle like hers wasn't held together by hope and good wishes, but by hairspray. She picked out some errant coloured paper that had clung tenaciously to her, dropping it on the sideboard.

'I'm surprised that you opted for confetti,' she said.

'Why?'

'It's messy.'

'I don't mind messy, in its place. Life's messy.'

There seemed to be weight to his words, but what was your wedding day if not a momentous occasion? Even though theirs was strictly business, it still carried a certain gravitas. That sensation pressed down upon her again, but she wouldn't dwell on it. Instead, Simone thought about the money in her bank account. Seven figures settled on her the moment she said *I do*. That amount would allow her to protect her sister Holly, who'd been abandoned by her parents because, like Simone, she hadn't fitted into the mould they'd tried to create for her.

Today ensured that the medical bills for Holly's increasingly complicated pregnancy, that she'd hidden till she couldn't any longer, were paid. That was all that mattered.

'I don't believe you've had a messy day in your life. You're all about the perfection. *Leo Zanetti never misses.*

Isn't that what everyone says about you? And never forget, I hear the complaints your suppliers and others have about you. Your exacting standards. As your EA, I hear it *all*.'

A look flashed across his face, almost like a wince, then it was gone.

'Then you've discovered my secret. The real reason for handing out confetti.'

'What?'

'It allowed people to throw things at me. Make them feel better about the *exacting standards* I impose upon them. Think of it as relationship building.'

The comment was so startlingly ridiculous a laugh simply burst from her, as she thought of their leaving the reception in an entirely different light. People hurling confetti whilst muttering, *take that, Leo Zanetti, for the time you told me I had the colour wrong, and it should have been Pantone 654 instead of Pantone 655, so you demanded we repaint twenty walls...*

Her eyes burned and blurred but at least her mascara was waterproof so she wouldn't end up looking like a Panda. Leo grinned. She could barely see it through her tears of mirth, but she could now tell the difference between the smile he flashed to his adoring public and the one he kept for private. The genuine smile. Relaxed, not studied.

This one was of the second sort. The private smile. She knew because it met his eyes and because of her reaction to it. Seeing that smile was like walking into the sunshine on a fine spring day, warm and satisfying.

'I'm pleased I could entertain you at my expense.'

'What good would you be as an employer if you

couldn't entertain me? Though admittedly that usually happens when you're not looking,' she said.

He raised a strong, inky eyebrow. 'Aren't I giving you enough work? When do you have time to appreciate this entertainment? I'm imagining it now. A cabal of executive assistants all mocking their employers behind their backs.'

'That's secret EA business and I'll never tell.' Simone tapped the side of her nose, her finger coming away damp from her tears of laughter. The truth was that she kept everything about Leo's business entirely confidential, as he well knew given her employment contract with its comprehensive confidentiality clauses.

His eyes narrowed, attempting to look stern but failing because the quirk at the corners of his perfect mouth remained. 'What would you all talk about?'

'I don't know. About the time you told a supplier you needed *a slightly warmer shade of black*?'

That conversation had involved a lengthy exchange of *warmer, cooler, getting closer* like some game of Hot and Cold hide and seek. She started giggling even harder.

'They weren't listening and were wasting my time. That job won *awards* because we got it right. I'm beginning to think you're unserious about Circolo's reputation. That's troubling. Why did I marry you again?'

'I don't know, Mr Zanetti. Perhaps you should read one of your press releases or interviews on the subject. Or would you prefer I do that for you and give you a precis, so that you're not wasting your time?'

Leo muttered something that sounded a lot like *incorrigible*. She was about to retort, *you love it* but held back because that would be a weird thing to say.

Whilst she'd always stood up for herself, stood up to him, their conversation had never been quite like this. So…familiar. Instead, Simone wiped at her eyes. When had she last laughed so hard that she cried? She couldn't remember, meaning it had to have been years. A thought that struck her as almost sad.

Leo reached his hand into the inner pocket of his tux, removed something with a flourish and held it out to her. She took it. It was a warm, pristine, white square of folded fabric.

'A handkerchief? How old school of you.' Simone dabbed at her eyes. Closed them, took a deep breath. The fabric smelled like him. His aftershave. Like spices and vanilla with a hint of rum. An intoxicating scent invoking memories of wintry Christmases and hot desserts. The excitement of unwrapping gifts. Something so nostalgic and familiar a yawning chasm just opened in her belly and she *yearned*.

'Someone needed to be prepared,' he said, breaking the spell that seemed to have been cast over her. 'Little did I understand the tears today wouldn't be about our getting married, but at my expense.'

'What good's a wife if not to tease her husband? I've heard we're all doing it and I'm trying really hard for authenticity here.'

'Clearly you're succeeding. Your act's entirely believable. The Tessitores will never think otherwise.'

She'd needed to get away from all the weird feelings that seemed to have overtaken her and hadn't known how. Thankfully, Leo had done it for her. Reminding them both of the truth of this arrangement. To help him win a business deal from people who didn't seem to understand or appreciate him. Apparently concerned about the number of women he'd been seen with in the press and what that meant for his stability, when Simone had little doubt that most women on the planet would want to be seen on his arm.

Plus, he *made* careers. Leo would date a model and then she'd be booked for months. Be seen having dinner with an up-and-coming designer of any sort? Their catalogue would be sold out overnight.

Really, Simone wondered why Leo was so intent on acquiring this company whose owners didn't seem to recognise his worth, even though he'd told her it was a heritage firm and part of the cultural fabric of the Lombardy region of Italy, which he wished to preserve. Of course, what Leonardo Zanetti wanted he got. She guessed this was just more of the same.

She balled up his handkerchief and held it out to him. 'Thank you. I'm fine now. My composure's firmly back in place.'

He waved her away. 'Keep it. In case there are any other moments where you lose your composure because of me. As your dutiful husband, I want to ensure I look after you. And on that point, whilst I offered you a drink I still haven't made you one.'

Simone hadn't had anyone looking after her since she'd walked away from her family seven years ago, at age twenty. At least she had her freedom now. She looked down at her wedding and engagement rings, glittering in the soft light of the room. When Leo had asked what style of ring she'd like and if she had a preferred colour of gem, she'd told him it didn't matter. Her only stipulation had been that she didn't want anything too ostentatious.

He didn't plant a country-sized boulder on her finger as she'd feared he might want to do. What he'd delivered was a round, two-carat diamond set in a platinum band. Not too big, as she'd asked. However, the diamond was an uncommon gem, internally flawless. And bisecting the band sat a fine channel lined with a circle of tiny, sparkling pastel gemstones that made a watercolour rainbow round her finger. Her wedding ring matched. She hadn't picked a single colour, so he gave her every one of them.

Simone wasn't sure why something in her chest ached as she looked at it. She shook it off. In the end, Simone guessed her rings were symbols of the loss of freedom she'd so craved. But at least they were put there as a result of her own choosing, rather than her parents'.

'Nice that you finally remembered. I wondered why I was feeling thirsty. What do you have?' she said as she made her way to an oversized lounge suite. She sank down into the plush cushions and wiggled her toes in the shoes she'd worn, which had been handmade to match the era of her gown.

She loved shoes. They were her only weakness. She'd had an unreasonable collection in her other life, before she'd realised that none of it mattered and one pair might have kept a family's bills paid and food on the table for a month. But these shoes… Covered in satin to match her gown, with magnificent handmade, wax citrus flowers to match the real blossoms in her bouquet that had been gathered into a little cluster as an embellishment at the front of each shoe. Just like an original thirties pair of shoes might have had. Delicate and perfect.

'You can have whatever your heart desires. However, I asked for a hazelnut liqueur to be placed in the suite for you,' Leo said, making his way to a credenza and holding up a shapely bottle full of amber fluid.

Simone's traitorous heart skipped a little beat and she rubbed the centre of her chest, settling the flutter there, that had struck like moths to lamplight. Leo knew she adored hazelnuts. Once he'd found out just how much she loved them, for the past two Christmases he'd given her a box of exquisite, handmade Belgian chocolates with hazelnut praline as a gift, along with her generous bonus, and she'd savoured them.

'*Perfetto*,' she said and he stilled, cocking his head, those vivid eyes of his fixed on her with the intensity of a spotlight making her want to squirm in her seat. 'What are you having?'

He began to pour her drink first into a lowball glass with ice. He reached into the bar fridge for his own, pouring the straw-coloured liquid into a tulip-shaped glass.

'Grappa,' Leo said as he strolled towards her, with a lazy roll of his hips, drinks in hand. He held out hers and she reached out to take it, their fingers touching. The moment was unintentional, she was sure, but she still tingled at the brush of his warm, tanned skin on hers. The moment had become strangely electric. The grip on her glass was tenuous, so she held on more tightly.

She wanted to say thank you, but her voice had been stolen so she smiled at him instead. Their gazes held and his nostrils flared. The moment shockingly potent. Simone was transported back to their time on the dance floor. Their bodies close, moving as one in an intoxicating synchronicity. The way his thumb hypnotically stroked the gleaming satin of her dress at her side. Simone didn't want to think about it, or to dwell. It had to be the whirlwind engagement and getting swept up in the day. That was all it was. Clearly her romantic fantasies hadn't quite left her when faced with their current and strange reality of this marriage of convenience. Even if she'd learned from painful experience that love was meaningless and easily bought off. But today wasn't really for lingering on past hurts. It was all about navigating her future. She took a small sip of her drink, the sweet nutty flavour sliding over her tongue.

'Are you sure about the absence of your family today? Not even your sister?'

The words caught her mid swallow. She forced her drink down, her eyes watering, trying not to cough. 'Why ask the question now, when the day's over?'

He hadn't shown much interest before and had accepted without comment that she didn't have anyone she wanted to invite. His attention now was strange and unsettling.

Leo didn't answer her immediately. He placed his drink down on an occasional table beside him. He shrugged out of his jacket and draped it carefully over an armchair, then sat on the couch at the other end from her. He tugged his bowtie undone, unfastened the top two studs of his dress shirt, then simply sprawled in the chair. He looked magnificently indolent, though she knew him better than that.

'I'm curious now,' he said, retrieving and sipping his drink. He held his glass almost negligently in his elegant hand, whereas she now gripped hers so tightly she feared she might crack it.

Some people might have likened him to a housecat in that moment, the way he lounged with a lazy expression. His eyes hooded, almost sleepy. The corners of his generous lips quirked into a sardonic kind of smile that had been written about and dissected by too many fashion commentators to be at all sensible or logical. Yet she'd never make the mistake of thinking of him as anything other than a panther, waiting for the perfect moment to pounce.

The more casual Leo appeared, the more watchful you had to be.

Simone had seen him like this before, when a new subcontractor hadn't done their job, having been lulled into a false sense of security that he was so laid back they could get away with shortcuts, only to be trapped by the inevitable attack on their workmanship that they hadn't seen coming.

People soon learned he could ruin them with an offhand comment. That's when they all fell into line. It was an incredible power he held. Yet she wouldn't let him wield it over her. People, like her parents, had tried before. Everyone had failed.

She shrugged, trying to match his casual attitude whilst inside it felt as if she was tangled in complicated knots. 'I'm certain. My sister hasn't been well and as for the rest… You know what families are like.'

Hers had seen fit to pay off her boyfriend. She'd met Jace at college. He was someone she'd known that her parents wouldn't have approved of, but that hadn't mattered at the time. Who cared that he was a boy that people might have said was from the wrong side of the tracks? He'd made good and had been awarded entry on a partial scholarship. Simone had admired him for it. Jace had chased her. Courted her. Acted like he respected her.

Showered her with attention that her emotion starved little heart had soaked up like parched earth on a rainy day. All her life she'd been taught to wait till she was married before sleeping with someone and, in her naivety, Simone believed that's what she'd wanted too. But on meeting Jace she'd questioned everything she'd once believed. Why would she have waited to sleep with him when he said he loved her? They'd planned a future together.

Even now, she didn't know what had been fake and what had been real. People claimed he'd been spreading stories about her. How simple it was to get her into bed. How he'd corrupted the poor little rich girl. Made jokes about it. And maybe that was true. Simone took a deep, slow breath. It might have been eight years ago, but it still ached like the wound was fresh. A knife to her tender heart that had never recovered. She blinked back the burn in her eyes because Leo would notice and he'd never get this part of her, that humiliation.

She'd learned a few things back then. How fickle her friends were. How they'd laughed behind her back for picking the poor kid to date. About how she'd *fallen*. Other boys in their group, sons of family friends she'd known since she'd been a child, had tried to come onto her because she'd apparently become fair game. A woman who could be fooled into bed. An easy mark.

The only thing she was sure about was how her parents had paid Jace off. Not for her own good, to save their beloved daughter, but to add to her humiliation. To show how easily they could wield their money to buy someone, especially when they threw it back in her face. Calling her home as if she was some kind of disgrace because she'd committed the sin of being talked about, rather than a heartbroken girl who needed their support. Showing her how little she was worth to the man she'd believed she'd marry one day, because they'd made promises to each other and she'd trusted them.

Simone realised then, that her relationship with her parents was entirely transactional. Her mom and dad cared more about their reputation than her. Even her brother had berated her, as if he was some scion of virtue when he'd slept his way through a swathe of girls, both in high school and in his own college years. It was then she'd decided to make her own way. The betrayal of her family was too great, their disdain of her impossible to bear. When she finally stood up for herself and said she didn't want what her parents demanded she accept as her life, they'd turned their backs. So, she'd walked away from it all, even Holly. Their relationship suffered because Holly was too young to understand why her big sister was leaving. That estrangement only really changed when her sister fell pregnant and recognised what Simone might have gone through. Getting in touch after eight long years of silence.

In all of this, the irony wasn't lost on Simone that she was now married to the kind of man her parents might have dreamed of for her. His wealth manifestly eclipsing theirs and all of their friends combined, even if he didn't have generations of illustrious family connections and old money behind him.

He was entirely self-made.

'Since I don't have a family, you might be surprised,' he said drawing her from a time she'd rather forget.

His past had been well ventilated in the press, though she was less interested in how Leo had been discovered by a modelling talent scout and more in how he'd survived when he'd been left with nothing. Born to a single mother, an artist and designer. Ending up on the streets as a teen, alone and hungry. His mother dying when he was barely an adult.

She hated thinking of that young man struggling to survive, which was why she was so determined for Holly to be protected. When she'd left home, she'd been lucky. Finding employment as an office junior. Working her way up in the company to become an executive assistant before leaving with an impeccable reference.

Not everyone had that kind of luck or those advantages.

'I didn't want what my parents wanted for me. They weren't happy about that. It's not an uncommon story,' she explained briefly. He didn't need any more of her sorry story.

'Then I'm surprised you didn't invite them to show them what you've achieved despite them.'

The only person she'd wanted here was Holly, but her doctors couldn't recommend she fly. Her placenta was low lying and she'd been bleeding. Holly also had higher than normal blood pressure. The constant threat of those complications meant it wasn't safe to travel and a lot of the time she needed bed rest.

'I have nothing to prove to people I'm wholly disinterested in. They don't need my emotional energy.'

'An admirable sentiment.'

Leo raised his glass to her. Like he'd raised it to her during his speech.

To my bride, who seems to have surprised everyone, but humbled me, by accepting my proposal.

There'd been chuckles in the crowd at that, even though Simone doubted Leo did much of anything, without knowing the answer first.

As for their engagement? There was no surprise about it at all. She'd been desperate to help Holly after they'd reconnected. Even with Simone's generous wage the medical bills were becoming crippling. She hadn't really thought about Leo's situation at all, given she never wanted to marry and Leo was her boss, until he'd uttered the fateful words in his office one day after yet another failed attempt at finding the right bride. After he asked why it couldn't be her, she'd immediately asked herself the same question.

Simone had known the eyewatering amount he was prepared to offer in his pre-nuptial agreement. It was enough to pay for an apartment in California for Holly. Her medical care. A nurse on call to visit whenever needed. Set things up for Holly and the baby. She could give her sister what Simone hadn't had for herself.

A soft place to land.

'Don't tell me you don't do the same to people who aren't important to you any more.'

The corner of his mouth kicked up. 'We're alike in that way, you and I. Were you at least happy with how it went today?'

Not so alike that their differences wouldn't keep pushing them apart like the same poles of a magnet. Yet if she was honest with herself, this had been the perfect wedding. Not for the teenage girl she once was, but the woman she'd become, even if she'd decided that love wasn't for her. From the intimate setting to the elegantly appointed room with whimsical floral centrepieces spilling from tall stands at each table's centre. The magnificent, tiered cake of different flavours, including chocolate hazelnut torte especially for her, decorated with cascades of blowsy sugar roses and tiny citrus blossoms that matched those in her bouquet. Leo's speech, which was strangely sentimental and delivered to warm applause.

The man knew how to please a crowd. It seemed like the whole day had been designed to make her happy.

'Yes, I was. Thank you. But with that, I'm going to turn in. It's been a long day.'

One she needed to process. Sift through. And she also needed to text Holly because Simone wanted to make sure her sister knew everything was okay. Wanted to send her photos of how beautiful everything had looked, since she'd expressed some suspicion as to what exactly was going on between Simone and Leo.

'Do you need any help with your dress?'

It was a benign kind of question and the look on his face seemed genuine enough, but something about today had been charged, a little electric. Hard to escape. The beautiful, silky dress that caressed her skin like a lover's touch. Leo, looking more handsome than any man had a right to be. The way he'd held her in his arms as they'd danced. She seemed to be enjoying the fantasy of the day a little too much.

But life wasn't a fantasy. She'd lived the end of hers. Jace's rejection. Taking money instead of a life with her. Her parents' disapproval. Her friends' disdain for and ridicule of her falling in love outside of her class.

Holly was living a kind of nightmare now too. Pregnant, unmarried. Once Simone had craved a loving family, one who accepted your failings. Embraced you and helped you through life. But that wasn't the world she'd come from and Leo represented everything that she'd left behind. A life she'd rejected because she'd realised it would never fit her. One where people cared more about how you appeared than who you really were and Leo was the *king* of appearances.

The Sultan of Style.

Simone stood and so did Leo. He was unfailingly polite that way. His manners impeccable. *Everything* about him impeccable when her life was really a bit of a mess. And whilst Leo claimed to like messy, she didn't believe him for a moment.

'No, thanks.'

'It has quite a few inconveniently placed buttons,' he pointed out.

A myriad of tiny satin covered ones down her side. It would be easier if someone undid them for her. She now had a sixth sense for bad intentions, having batted off a few CEOs who'd thought being their assistant at their beck and call meant in *every* way. Leo didn't give off those vibes. He never had. Their parameters were clear. For her, this was a job like any other. He'd promised her the same. Simone shook her head as he looked down on her with those famed eyes of his. Transfixed in a shade of blue the colour of a tropical sea.

'I got myself into this, I'll get myself out of it.'

CHAPTER THREE

It HAD BEEN an eight-hour flight from New York to Milan on Leo's private jet. Simone had tried to sleep on the way in the stateroom at the back, given they'd left in the early evening and flown through the night, but all she'd done was toss and turn. Much like she had in New York. After she'd sent Holly some pictures hastily snapped of the venue, Simone had finally had time to replay the wedding and reception, recognising how much effort Leo had put into getting everything right. It was no less than she'd expected from him, but the day had been a whirlwind where she hadn't had time to think about the things that Leo had *no* control over. In bed on her own, on her wedding night in their suite, she finally had. How she'd felt like a different woman under the intensity of Leo's gaze. The sensation of being cradled in his arms on the dance floor, their bodies close, like she'd always imagined when she'd fantasised about being married for real.

A flush of heat washed over her.

When she'd agreed to this arrangement, Simone hadn't much thought about how it might affect her as she'd been in the midst of panic after finding out about Holly's situation. She'd been desperate to protect her sister, who by coincidence was the same age as Simone had been when her own life had imploded. The sheer relief of knowing she could pay all of Holly's outstanding medical bills and keep her safe had then obliterated the logistics of what it meant to be Leo Zanetti's wife. Because it wasn't like being his executive assistant, at all.

In the lead up to the wedding it had been easy enough to be all smiles. Playing the game she once knew intimately. She'd been happy that with each stage towards their wedding another payment mandated by their prenuptial agreement came through. That she could find Holly an apartment, make sure her high risk pregnancy was monitored by the best available team. That all her sister needed to do now was to sit back and relax while her baby grew.

The difficulty was maintaining the fakery to everyone else when Simone had fought to live her life true to herself, with authenticity. It didn't sit well. Yet she tried reminding herself that getting married to Leo was a means to an end, not the end itself.

'I've been advised there are photographers outside the house,' Leo said from where he sat in the back of the car as they travelled to his home in a fashionable part of the city.

'Photographers follow you wherever you go.'

'A teaser of one of our wedding photos for the magazine spread dropped today. It's not me they're interested in.'

He shot her an unreadable look. Simone was dressed as she always was for a flight like this, when they weren't going straight into the office or a business meeting afterwards. A white collared shirt with casual black trousers. Her uniform. Something she didn't have to think about.

Yet she was thinking about it now. Was Leo judging her appearance? What might be written about her when the inevitable pictures hit the press?

In contrast, Leo looked stylish as ever with his casual elegance. *Sprezzatura* she'd heard it called, an almost careless perfection. Today he was dressed in buff tan chinos and similar toned loafers. A navy linen shirt with the sleeves rolled up. He'd strolled onto the tarmac after their flight carrying a worn and well-loved leather bag looking effortless and gloriously rumpled. If she didn't know better, she might have thought the flight attendant had fanned herself as they'd walked off the plane.

Simone almost did too.

'I see this as an opportunity,' Leo went on. 'Will that be a problem?'

'Depends on what opportunity you're talking about.'

'It'll be our first unofficial sighting in Italy, as husband and wife. I'll ask the driver to park out front rather than driving into the garage, so we can be seen walking into the home together.'

She understood what Leo meant now. Putting on a show. She sighed. They had a busy time in Italy. A few days in Milan where Leo had organised a mystery day out, then a dinner with the Tessitores to introduce Simone as his wife and hopefully discuss a possible purchase of their company. After that, they were heading off on a brief honeymoon in Verona, which she didn't need but realised was necessary to maintain the narrative their whole marriage was meant to portray. Then, they'd be going back to Milan, rounding off the Italy trip with a charity ball.

Simone rubbed her temple, the thought of it almost

enough to give her a headache. They were supposed to present as a loved-up couple fresh from their wedding and she had little idea how to portray that. Her only experience had been with Jace and she *refused* to think about that relationship. How would she even behave now, if really in love? Simone had no idea.

'Are we talking about simply walking in here? Something else?' Butterflies took wing in her belly, flapping about violently. Would he ask for a kiss? They didn't even kiss at the altar, he'd made her laugh instead… Her chest became tight and it was hard to—

'Breathe, Simone.'

She tried to relax. Took a breath as he'd asked. That almost made it worse because, as on the night of their wedding, Leo smelled *delicious*. She chanced a look at him. His lips quirked into a wry yet somewhat concerned smile. At her reaction no doubt. Leo wouldn't want his new wife swooning because she'd held her breath and fainted at the thought of getting up close and personal with him, even if it was only for show.

'As I said once before, you're bad for my ego.'

He'd completely misunderstood her inability to breathe and that was fine because she hardly understood it herself.

'All I'm asking is that we hold hands. Perhaps touch each other with affection till we get inside. I won't ever ask what you're not prepared to give.'

'So, we touch in a way that could potentially be judged as a breach of Circolo's *Working Together* policy but not in a way that mandates HR's immediate involvement.'

Leo laughed, his face lighting up with mirth and some element of self-deprecation.

'Since most women I've spent time with wish to touch me in a way that would flagrantly breach every HR policy available on Circolo's intranet, and even some decency laws, that'll do nicely.'

'Mr Zanetti, your ego clearly remains solidly intact. As I believe *I've* said once before.'

'Mrs Zanetti, my expectation is that you'll attempt to crush it with your ruthlessly efficient shoes at every given opportunity. It would worry me if you stopped trying.'

This would have been the perfect time for her to laugh too, to lighten the mood even further. Instead she glanced down at her black pumps. Boring. Practical. Ruthlessly efficient as he'd said. Simone wished she had another pair of shoes to wear. Like some towering, patent black heels because she loved patent leather, and they'd have added a bit of interest to her otherwise restrained, matte outfit...

'Are you happy with my suggestion?' Leo asked. What could she say? Simone nodded and he said something in Italian to the driver. The car changed course slightly, pulling into a side street. The street where his home was situated. Her heart jolted like a horse at a starting gate.

'Affectionate touching. Holding hands. Got it.'

The car slowed to a stop at the front of the house. A magnificent, semi-detached art deco villa. There wasn't far to go, a quick walk across the footpath to the front gate, then they'd be behind the vine-covered wall and away from prying eyes. Easy.

'The photographers are across the road. Wait till I open your door.'

Leo hopped out of the car and stood on the footpath waiting for her. The click of shutters sounded staccato to the left of their vehicle. Simone refused to look over towards them, even though they'd be unlikely to glimpse her through the tinted windows. She began to slide across the seat. Leo ducked his head to peer at her, then held out his hand as if to offer her some support. She took it, his grasp warm and strong as he helped her from the car.

Photographers called his name. *Leo! Mr Zanetti!* Then to her. *Simone, where's the honeymoon?* It was discombobulating, surreal, the world she'd been thrust into. Leo gathered her into him, against his hard body, ignoring the shouts from across the road. It was as if nothing else existed bar them. He leaned down so his lips were at her ear. His breath, a warm caress.

'Remember to breathe.'

Goosebumps shivered over her. Instead of pulling away, she melted in even further. Something about the role they'd slipped into suddenly became too easy. Seamless.

'Remember not to breach too many HR policies,' she whispered, a little breathless, despite his reminder. It was nerves, that was all. He was used to this. The man graced magazines covers, dated movie stars, walked red carpets. She was simply Simone Taylor.

Plain Jane.

Leo chuckled, throaty and deep. The sound rumbled right through her. 'I'd never dream of it.'

Leo threaded his fingers through hers and squeezed, then walked with her towards the tall, wrought iron gate that led to his property, ushering her through and locking it behind them. They crossed the small front garden and marbled terrace area with its potted olive trees, then through the front door and into the house.

That's where the closeness ended. He disentangled himself from her and she strangely mourned the loss of all his warmth and strength. It had felt good, having him talking her through, being able to rely on him.

Now, he was all business.

'I'm sure you'd like to see your room.'

She'd been in Leo's magnificent Milan property before. One of the few people privileged to see the living areas on the ground floor at least. Not many people had. Whilst style magazines gushed over his other residences that were dotted around the world, he'd never invited them into this one. The only photographs of it available online, were old real estate listings before he'd purchased it and done an extensive renovation. Whilst the palette of the villa was all warm neutrals, from the glorious, honey-eyed floorboards to the creamy walls, the spaces were punctuated with pops of colour. From the large antique rugs on the floor to the soft furnishings and art on the walls. It was a place that looked…inviting. Loved. Lived in. Unlike his more modern interiors, which struck her as showpieces, this one had history about it. It felt more like Leo than any other place she'd seen.

Like home.

Instead of heading into the lounge area Leo made his way up a flight of stairs to the upper floor, then up another flight to what appeared to be an attic area.

'I've given you the whole top floor. I thought you might appreciate the privacy. The main bedroom's below you.' He opened the door and walked in. She followed.

The space stole her breath. It was unlike any other part of the house she'd seen. Once Leo had asked Simone her favourite colour and she'd said she had none, probably more in a fit of rebellion than anything else. This room, *her* room, was entirely decorated in shades of white and cream. It should have looked cold, soulless, but the space was anything but that. The ceilings were ornately moulded plasterwork.

Against one wall was a four-poster bed in a pale, whitewashed wood. The covers were plush and soft and it was stacked with pillows that looked like you could sink into them and never want to leave. The canopy and drapes were filmy and light, tied back against the posts, giving the room an understated opulence. A velvet covered bench sat at the end of the bed.

Along a wall opposite to the bed sat a large couch in an off-white linen with matching cushions. It was a space designed for someone to inject their personality should they wish, yet still felt complete just as it was, an elegantly conceived blank canvas.

Designed by someone who'd listened to her.

'This is glorious,' she whispered, her eyes burning with emotion at Leo's thoughtfulness. Her own room in her old family home had been decorated by an interior designer. What Simone had wanted hadn't really factored into the plan at all. Her mother had demanded the space match the rest of the house and so Simone had always thought it was cold and soulless.

This room was none of those things.

'I hope you'll be comfortable here,' Leo said.

'I know I will.'

She couldn't look at him right now, because if she did, she might be totally overcome by it all. Instead, she moved to one of the windows set into the sloping ceiling and pulled back the filmy curtain. Below them sat a walled garden, a slice of green with lush plantings and what appeared to be a huge magnolia tree in the back corner, which would look magnificent when it flowered.

'Is there anything you need?' Leo asked.

All Simone needed was time to regroup. She shook her head. 'I think you've done more than enough.'

She turned and tried to smile but it felt weak and shaky. Leo didn't seem to notice. Nothing about his demeanour changed, apart from looking a little pleased with himself.

'As you've done for me. Don't think your efforts are unappreciated. For this morning, I have some work to do—'

'Can I help?' Work. That's what she needed to get back her equilibrium. It reminded her of what her role really was here, as his valued executive assistant.

Leo shook his head. 'It shouldn't take long. Something a little time sensitive is all.'

That of itself was strange. Disappointment settled like a stone in her stomach. Simone knew everything about his work and she'd seen nothing on her email indicating anything time sensitive had come in. There was also something a bit different about Leo in this moment. He appeared a little closed off. Though perhaps the 'work' had something to do with the 'surprise' he'd scheduled in for tomorrow.

'I also realise the only time you've seen Milan is for your job, so if you'd like me to take you sightseeing after I'm done...'

Simone didn't need more time in close proximity to Leo, not after this. And especially not with the risk of photographers following them to capture every glaring detail without the time to prepare herself. What she really needed was space and sleep. Perhaps if she was a little better rested her head would clear. At the moment, her thoughts and emotions were a complicated tangle she needed to undo.

'Maybe another time,' she said. 'I'd like to catch up with my sister this afternoon. Give her a call and see how she is.'

'Of course.' Leo hesitated. Slipped his phone from his pocket and checked it. Frowned. Tapped a quick message. Pressed send. Returned his gaze to hers with a tight smile. Clearly he wasn't happy about something. She might have asked what, but if he wanted to tell her he would. 'Your bags will be up soon. Remember our day trip tomorrow. Dress—'

'For a day on the water. I remember. I packed appropriately.'

'Of that, *cara*, I have no doubt. I'll let you get settled.' He gave her a sharp nod, then turned and left the room. Alone with her thoughts, doubting everything.

Leo motored the boat he'd hired across Lake Garda. The breeze cool and fresh over the vivid blue water. His mother had always spoken fondly of growing up around this place, before moving to Milan and meeting his father. An idyllic childhood in a little village, swimming on the lake, catering to tourists. They'd been back to Lake Garda a few times when he was a child, but then the family furniture business had taken over and consumed everything. He'd wondered whether his mother had felt landlocked, moving away from the water and a place she'd loved so much.

He'd always regretted that he'd never thought to ask.

Leo ignored the sensation, one that had plagued him unrelentingly in the years since his mother had died. Today wasn't about that past, but the present.

'You've been the international man of mystery today,' Simone said. 'Where are we going?'

'You'll see.'

'That's not helpful.'

Leo winked. 'I recommend living in the moment. Trust me.'

Simone's cheeks seemed to flush a gratifying shade of pink, a reaction he enjoyed a little too much. Of course, it could also have been the sun radiating warmth against her skin.

The purpose of today had been two-fold. He'd thought Simone might enjoy some time exploring one of the area's natural treasures. Then there was their impending dinner with the Tessitores. His marketing manager reported that the Silvestris had been wining and dining the family at some of Milan's finest venues. Acid burned in Leo's gut and he gritted his teeth. It was imperative their dinner tomorrow was successful and yet Simone remained a little reticent around him. Moments of trust and closeness like when the paparazzi had been photographing them and she'd sunk into his arms, then moments of pulling away. It was enough to fool the public in a photograph, likely not enough in a more intimate setting as the dinner would be. They needed something more. To cement an understanding between them that they hadn't truly achieved as employer and employee.

Today was meant to be fun, enjoyable. Reaching a

kind of familiarity with one another, when to date they'd only ever been about work.

'Would it help if I told you we're visiting a place not open to the public, owned by one of my clients?'

'You mixing work with pleasure doesn't surprise me at all. That's who you are.'

The comment stung, even though it was fair. But in the end, it had been his desire never to be cold or hungry again that drove him to succeed where so many others had failed. Whilst there were a thousand things he needed to atone for, he wouldn't apologise for that.

Leo steered the vintage wooden motor launch towards a private jetty just visible in the distance. Simone matched the vibe of the day without even realising it. In white canvas shorts and a pretty blue and white polka-dot top. Her hair in a high ponytail, tied with a blue scarf. Wearing sneakers in a blue and white polka dot too, a hint of whimsy that surprised him given she always seemed buttoned up so tight. Add in some oversized sunglasses and a beachy looking wicker and leather bag and she looked like the perfect sixties starlet. He wondered what the fashion magazines might say about her today? They'd likely think the same as him in this moment.

She was perfect.

It shocked him that for two years he hadn't really noticed her appearance at all when now, he had trouble looking away. There was far more to Simone than she'd ever let on in the office. The woman had been as cool and opaque as the finest Carrara marble. Yet for him, he would only be able to admire from afar. Whilst Leo believed she enjoyed him telling her she was beautiful, their interactions would remain forever distant because that's what she wanted. So did he. Not to ruin a perfect working relationship or risk the deal with Tessitore he so fervently desired.

'Are you going to give me even a teensy hint of what's so special?'

'There,' he pointed as the historic villa came into view, rising above the treetops beside the lake. Its famed terraced gardens now obvious.

'Wow.'

That was a common reaction. The house was passed by most boating tours of the lake and was a favourite with its classical style of columns and arches. However, the true treasure of the place wasn't the house, as magnificent as it was, but the natural wonder the gardens held.

He pulled the launch up to the private jetty and jumped out, tying up the boat. Then he turned. Simone stood looking down at him as if getting ready to jump down herself.

'Let me help you,' he said.

'Oh. Sure.'

Leo reached up, his hands spanning her slender waist. Taking her weight as she hopped down. Their bodies close, closer. She didn't appear to be moving, like the day seemed to have paused on this moment. He should let her go, yet why didn't he want to?

'You okay?' he asked instead.

He was just steadying her, that was all. Her lips parted as if Simone was trying to take in more air. He wished he could see her eyes. How stormy grey they were in this moment, which seemed charged with something electric.

'Signor and Signora Zanetti. Welcome!'

The voice came from behind him. Leo released Simone and she swayed a little. He gently took her elbow and turned to see a man striding down the dock.

'My name's Guido and I'm the caretaker. I hope you both had a good journey?'

Leo shook the man's hand and Simone smiled. She made such a glorious picture against the vibrancy of the lake, her blonde hair gleaming like gold in the sunshine.

'I don't think I can imagine anywhere much more beautiful,' she said, looking around out over the water, up towards the house.

'Then it's my pleasure to welcome you here today. We have some refreshments, which will be served at the gazebo overlooking the lake. Would you like them now, or a little later?'

Leo looked over at Simone, his eyes raised, and she shook her head.

'*Grazie*, later,' he said. 'We'll explore some of the gardens first.'

'It's a good time to visit, we've had recent rains. The grounds are open to you for as long as you wish today. Should you need assistance, please ask one of the staff or come to my office. It's in an outbuilding near the house. I'll be here all day.'

The man waved and went on his way as they followed along the jetty till they reached a paved promenade stretching along the waterfront.

'Where to now?' she asked, the charged moment on the dock seemingly forgotten, by her at least.

'Pick a direction. There's no bad choice and we have plenty of time.'

Simone hesitated then turned left, the pathway taking them up through a series of garden rooms. From towering trees near the waterfront like some ancient forest, walking through to a riot of annual flowers, morphing into a wild looking meadow garden. Prizewinning and world-renowned, the only place most people other than a privileged few, would ever see all this beauty, was in photographs. As they moved further up the hillside the sound caught his ears. Rushing water. Although if you didn't know where the path led, you might mistake it for the sound of wind in the trees.

'What *is* this place?' Simone asked, stopping at a particularly beautiful view, framed by clipped olive trees and huge pots spilling over with red geraniums. Simone removed her sunglasses in the shade of the trees, took her phone out of her bag and snapped a photograph, slipping the phone into the pocket of her shorts.

'A privately owned residence. I helped the owner source some items for a renovation after he'd inherited it. Building a pavilion.'

'Are the owners here?'

'It's not the family's main residence. They spend most of the year out of Italy.'

'Why would you own this and not live here?'

'I have homes all over the world that I don't spend much time in.'

Though Leo was inclined to agree about this place. Its beauty needed to be experienced, not hidden away. When he'd come to know the place, he'd offered to buy it. The owner wouldn't sell, although they'd struck up a friendship and his client had said Leo could come back to visit. For Simone, Leo had called in the favour.

She rolled her eyes. No one else would have dared but

he'd always enjoyed her sass. 'You forget. I know your property portfolio and you don't have *anything* like this.'

Simone was the only woman on the planet who might leave him feeling a little chastened.

'Are you trying to make me feel inadequate because of the size and breadth of my personal real estate?'

She cocked her head, her cool grey gaze almost assessing. The slightest wash of pink drifted across her cheeks again.

'I think you're doing just fine on the personal real estate front, Leo.'

The comment could have been innocent. It could also have meant something else entirely. The former was the safe conclusion. The latter, far more enticing.

Simone blew out a breath in a huff, lifting some stray hairs falling to her face. She brushed them out of the way, then she turned and kept walking like he'd been dismissed. It didn't matter. They were getting close to the place that held the real magic of the home. His heart beat a little faster. What would she think when she saw it?

She stopped at another beautiful view. Pink nerium vivid against the backdrop of the blue lake. Simone slipped her phone out of her pocket and took another photograph. There was something about her wanting memories that pleased him.

She turned to look at him, a slight frown creasing her brow. 'Do you want a selfie together? To show us in wedded bliss?'

He'd never taken a selfie in his life. 'Where would we post it? I don't do personal socials.'

There were enough fan sites extolling his imagined and not so imagined virtues. He didn't have the time or inclination to do anything more. His business sites were carefully managed by his marketing department. He supposed Simone could have posted something on hers, if she had any. Except when he and Simone had made the decision to marry, his marketing department suggested she make her own sites private. She'd told them she had none.

Simone Taylor was a ghost. A mystery.

She nibbled on her bottom lip. 'Send it to PR and see what they say.'

There was something about her, a little uncertain. He wondered whether it wasn't PR she was thinking of for the photograph, but herself. Once again, that pleased him in a way that was entirely foreign.

'Good idea. Then we'll let them decide.'

They positioned themselves with the magnificent view as a backdrop. Simone with her arm out, trying to catch the shot. It felt awkward, stilted like this. He guessed it would look even worse if it was ever shown to the public.

'My arms are longer, how about I take it?' he offered.

'Sure, why not.' She handed him her phone, warm from her touch. He purposely didn't think about how that warmth seeped into his palm as he held out the phone and they moved close. Her smile didn't seem genuine, her lips a little tight, which wouldn't do. He could give a winning smile, a money shot, on muscle memory alone.

'Say, Taleggio.'

'Why would I say that?'

'Taleggio's my favourite cheese.'

Her eyes widened and then she laughed. It was such a bright, joyful sound. Like birds waking at dawn. He smiled at the thought and took the photograph, then a few more for good measure.

The bare skin of her arm was soft against his own. She smelled like the citrus blossom that flowered everywhere at this time of the year. He didn't want to move, but they couldn't stand here like this any longer.

'I think that's enough to work with. Take a look.'

He handed back the phone. Simone scrolled through the pictures, looked up at him with a soft smile on her face.

'They're fantastic. Honestly, I don't think there could ever be a bad photograph of you.'

Leo rarely thought about his own looks, despite his stratospheric modelling career. His face was nothing more than an accident of DNA. However, Simone's simple comment sent a curl of pleasure through him.

'Why Mrs Zanetti, are you handing me a compliment?'

'It's my job as your wife to keep you grounded, so I'd never do that.' The corner of her lips tilted into a sly smile. 'You get far too many anyway. One more would be superfluous.'

'I don't like the way you keep imposing gravity upon me.'

'You're a highflyer. I'm just trying to keep your feet on the ground occasionally. Remind you what life's like, being a mere mortal like me.'

Her comment was an innocent one, said in a moment of fun, but it took him back to a time when he'd felt all too mortal. One he didn't want to remember, not today. The breeze changed and the sound from before became louder. Unmistakeable.

'What's that noise?' Simone asked, looking up the hill in its direction.

'The real wonder of this place,' he smiled, his heart rate picking up with anticipation. He wanted her to enjoy this, be struck by the wonder of it as he'd first been. 'Come on, this way takes us through the arid garden which is a bit rocky.'

He held out his hand to her and she slipped hers into it with no hesitation. They moved upwards, through the gravel paths and boulders, passing succulents and cactus, then onwards as the atmosphere began changing. Tree ferns dotted the space, the undergrowth lush. The air here cooler, more humid, almost like they'd been transported into a rainforest. The rush of water became even more pronounced as they rounded a corner.

Simone turned to him, her mouth open in wonder. 'Is that what I think it is?' Her voice was louder because the sound was now unmistakeable. The rush of water turning into a roar.

Ahead the hillside rose to their left and the path led through a grotto cut into the rock. But the wonder of it was that at the right time of the day, the mist that came from what was in the cave caught the light and a rainbow illuminated their way.

She let go of Leo's hand and hurried forwards, laughing as she took another photograph of the beauty and simplicity of white light shining through water droplets. He'd been all but forgotten, although that didn't matter. Her joy was all he'd craved to see and here he had it. He could take out his own phone and snap a picture of her smile, which would capture something more vibrant and beautiful than the misty rainbow ahead of him.

She disappeared into the dark fissure in the rock and he jogged to follow, not wanting to miss her reaction. He entered the space just behind her and she squealed. 'Oh my...look at this. Look. At. This.'

A waterfall cascaded through the rocks from above them, rushing under a stone bridge and away down the hillside to the lake. Simone stopped at the perfect vantage point, looking up from where the water roared over the hillside into the grotto where they stood, carefully placed artificial lighting accenting the space.

'It's so beautiful.' She shouted to be heard over the sound, far louder than when he'd been here before, clearly because of recent rains. 'I can't...'

Right now, with her smile as natural as the wonder surrounding him, she was the most beautiful thing here, without compare. She stood, gripping the railing. The mist from the waterfall drifted all round them and made their clothes damp the longer they stood here. Simone's pretty shirt began to cling to her body. Her nipples tight under the fine fabric. It was cooler here, that was all. Nothing more. His own polo was sticking to his body too. After a few more moments, Simone moved on, which was sensible because they were at risk of becoming drenched if they stood there too long.

'People should see this. People *need* to see this,' she said.

'Yet we're only two of the privileged few.'

'It pays to know you then, I guess.'

'I do come with some benefits.'

She caught him with her stormy gaze, her eyes flicking almost imperceptibly down his body then back up again. Most people wouldn't have noticed, but with her he saw everything.

Even in this cool hidden corner, heat speared through him potent and fiery. He craved to press her against the chill metal of the railings, kiss her. Hold her close. Hear her moan. There'd been no real kiss at the wedding. Only a peck on the cheek and whispered words in her ear to lighten the moment.

They believe we married for love, when I know you only married me for my choice of cake.

Her favourite flavour, one layer of chocolate hazelnut torte. That had made her laugh, which turned the moment from something that might have looked forced, to something warm and genuine.

Yet she'd made herself clear about not wanting anything further and in his vows he'd promised to honour her. Even if they were promises made in a fake marriage, he'd keep them. He'd spent his youth being dishonourable. He wanted to be honourable now, even though this seemed like a moment full of possibility and impossibility at the same time.

Leo clenched his hands, flexed his fingers. The urge to reach out, touch, hold. Seize the moment to see where it led, almost unbearable. He shut his eyes for a moment, took a deep breath. A reset.

'The property manager promised refreshments in the rotunda. It's a beautiful view there, one of the finest on the property.'

'Another beautiful view? How many can there be?'

Only one. Standing right in front of him, but that was something he couldn't admit.

'Countless,' he said to avoid the truth, in his own mind

at least. 'If you'd like, we could go there, then walk the gardens some more?'

'Th-that would be lovely.'

'How about I lead the way?'

Simone nodded and he walked on ahead, the path curving down into the sunshine, to where a gazebo sat, overlooking the lake. There was jug of what appeared to be fresh lemonade, water condensing on the side. A platter of antipasto and *piadina* under an insect cover. They sat at opposite sides of the solid wooden table in the shade and he poured a drink for each of them as they nibbled on the delicious food.

The mascara below Simone's eyes had smudged from the dampness, making her look soft. Her eyes appeared smoky, as they did on their wedding day when he felt as though he'd seen her for the first time. She pulled out her phone and flicked through her photos. He took the moment to check his own phone and wished he hadn't. More problems in Rome. Reminders of the Tessitore dinner. His gut clenched, the food sitting like a rock. He took a sip of his cold, lemony drink.

'You happy with this one?' Simone asked and brought up a photo of them laughing. It was a good picture. Natural. Joyous. 'I wouldn't mind sending it to my sister and maybe Marchesa too.'

Marchesa was Simone's assistant, who was doing her job whilst they were away. Simone had been reluctant when he'd first suggested she have help, until he'd reminded her that as his wife, she'd be taking on additional roles so might need someone to relieve her of the administrative work that was now above her pay grade.

'She can pass it on to PR for us. Saves people wondering why you're thinking of work on what's supposed to be your honeymoon. How is Holly?'

'She's…okay. Thanks for asking.'

Simone's brow creased in a small frown, as if she was surprised he might have cared. Yet it was a salutary reminder of the whole purpose for this marriage. Business, not pleasure. He needed to make that his mantra.

'Our dinner with the Tessitores tomorrow…'

Their first public outing and a shot across the Silvestri family's bow. Once he'd started modelling, built his business, he'd vowed never to allow anyone to take anything from him again. Owning this famed, heritage brand would cement his reputation and mess with his father and half-brother's plans. *Nothing* was more important.

'Mmm?' Simone popped an olive into her mouth. Her glossy lips wrapping round her fingers, licking off the marinade oil. A dart of desire rocketed through him, spearing low.

Business, not pleasure. Business, not pleasure.

Leo cleared his throat.

'There's a fine personal shopper in Milan should you want something to wear.'

Simone's gaze shot up from her phone screen. 'I won't embarrass you with my sartorial choices, if that's what you're worried about.'

'That's not what I—'

'Yes, you were. *Plain Jane.* That's what everyone calls me. Don't you like it, Leo? Do you think the title reflects badly on you, given everyone calls you the Sultan of Style? Because I'm not like them. I'm not obsessed with appearances instead of the person inside. I'm simply disinterested.'

She stood with her eyes narrowed. The cool grey burning hot with anger. He hadn't meant any of those things, yet this was like the rush of the waterfall, roaring over the rocks. He didn't know how to stop it.

'I'm aware—'

She glared at him, 'I'm not you, Leo. Don't try to turn me into someone I don't want to be. We had a deal. But if you're worried, I'm wearing the teal dress. The one you gave me.'

One he'd sourced with care when their engagement was announced. A dress he'd believed she'd find acceptable and, in her words, sustainable.

'The dress from our engagement's a nice touch,' he said, trying to repair what he'd clearly broken.

Simone crossed her arms, almost a protective move. 'I *know*. I thought it seemed sentimental. Now, I'm not so sure about anything. How about you stay here and eat so the effort the staff put in for us isn't wasted? I'm not hungry any more. I'm going to keep walking.'

Simone stalked off, taking a different path, rounding a corner and disappearing into the garden without looking back. Leo took a slow breath, trying to understand how quickly the moment had changed, from something wonderful, to this.

CHAPTER FOUR

SIMONE CHECKED HER PHONE. She'd finally sent Holly a picture of the villa she and Leo had visited the day before, their selfie, as reassurance that they were having a good time. Her sister's reply came quickly.

OMG amazing view followed by flame emojis.

She didn't think those flames were referring to the view in the background, admittedly amazing as it was.

Simone pulled up the photo again. Her, laughing. Leo's own grin, warm and generous. The corners of his eyes crinkling as if they'd just shared a secret joke. To someone who knew nothing about their relationship it would have told a story of a loving couple on their honeymoon. To her, it was a photo full of lies.

She put down her phone, satisfied that Holly was happy, and walked to the window of her room. Staring out onto the slice of garden lit up as night fell and then out to the city beyond. She mused about how life and moments could change in an instant, with only a word.

The day on Lake Garda and at the private waterfall had been a magical experience. Motoring at speed across the glorious water. The sun warm, the breeze cool. The planning it must have taken for Leo to arrange the day.

Not somewhere people could sightsee, but a private residence because he believed she might like it.

It had shown thought and care. Or at least, she'd believed it had. That it was a result of someone considering her desires, what she might actually enjoy, rather than what they wanted with her as a peripheral consideration. It had been wondrous, beautiful. Looking up at that waterfall tumbling over the rocks and rushing away underneath them, gleaming with perfectly positioned lights. Surrounded by the rock walls, covered in mosses and little ferns, it could have been something out of a fairy tale. A portal to another world where she and Leo were different people and a realm of possibility was open to them.

But as she needed to remember, she and Leo weren't different people. He was Leo Zanetti, wanted all over the world for how he looked. To set trends. She was his reliable EA, Simone Taylor. It was good that he'd reminded her of that. Sure, he probably thought he was being kind when he talked about what she was going to wear tonight. Whilst she tried not to care because it was all so meaningless, Simone didn't want to be thought of as *Plain Jane* either, even though she knew that wasn't who she was deep down.

People had called her beautiful once, when she was younger, and wore the 'right' clothes. The designer ones, with the glam makeup and hair that had been styled for hours by a hairdresser. It's just that that wasn't what was important about a person. It was who they were inside that mattered. She'd met some of the most beautiful people on the planet in her time—at college, socialising with her parents, through her role as an EA and espe-

cially with Leo. Some naturally endowed, others surgi-
cally enhanced. She didn't judge. What she'd come to
know was that beauty was subjective, but it was also a
meaningless measure of someone's worth. Especially
when some people were just plain ugly inside.

Well, if her outward appearance was what Leo was
worried about, there wasn't much she could do about
it. She'd made promises to herself about setting aside
frivolous things like clothes and makeup and she was
sticking to them. Simone checked the time. Tonight was
their dinner with the Tessitores. What this whole marriage was about. Whilst all she wanted to do was stay in
and eat a burger and a bowl of fries, Simone had a job
to do. She'd never shirked before and she wouldn't now.
But she wasn't interested in this game Leo was playing.
Her illusions felt a little shattered, the ground beneath
her somewhat unsteady. For one fleeting, ridiculous moment she'd believed Leo had been thinking about her
when he'd arranged that boat trip, when most likely, all
he was doing was buttering her up for the conversation
he wanted to have about how she was going to look on
his arm tonight.

It was like something inside her had been crushed
and killed. What did that say about her? That she was
so starved for attention she'd deluded herself into trying
to find it in a relationship that was completely transactional? She shook her head. It didn't matter. Right now,
her focus had to be on pretending to be an adoring wife.
That was her job. What she'd been employed to do.

She walked over to the mirror, peering at her reflection. Her hair was done up but not in her usual, tight,
shiny chignon. Instead, she was trialling a claw clip hack

video Holly had sent her, which was meant to be quick
and easy and without the need for so many hair pins. The
problem was that her hair wasn't quite behaving. Not
sleek like she preferred for business occasions as this
was. Tonight, little pieces of it were falling about her face
making the whole style a bit soft. A lot less like herself.

More like the girl she used to be.

Simone gave her makeup one last check, though why,
she wasn't sure. It was the same as always. Natural, with
her lips slicked with a little rosy gloss. She looked 'put
together', as some people might have called it, though not
high glamour, because that had never really been her, no
matter the box her parents had tried to squeeze her into.
And why she was thinking about them now, she didn't
know. Her whole life seemed completely topsy-turvy.
She needed to stop romanticising the trip on the boat,
stop thinking about her parents, and remember who she
was. Simone Taylor. A hard worker. A trustworthy and
trusted employee. A good person who was more interested in internal substance than external appearances.
And if people didn't like it, including Leo, then they
could, to put it colloquially, take a hike.

Simone grabbed her clutch and left her room, standing at the top of the stairs leading down to the second
level of the home where Leo's bedroom was. As she did,
he walked through his own door, his timing impeccable,
as always. Right now his head was down, checking his
phone in one hand. In his other, holding something she
couldn't really see. Seeing him, her breath caught. Her
heart speeding to a thready rhythm as it fluttered against
her ribs as if a kaleidoscope of butterflies had taken up
residence there. He was wearing a suit, like so many men

she'd worked with over the years, but Leonardo Zanetti wore a suit like nobody else. The way it hugged his broad shoulders, draped and shaped his body. His tie in a gorgeous check of teals and reds, complementing her dress to perfection. She squashed any lingering fantasy that his choice of tie showed he'd thought of her. Being who he was, she shouldn't have expected anything less.

Then he looked up at her and those piercing blue eyes of his stabbed right through Simone's chest. What did he see when he did that? It was impossible to tell, though his gaze did give her a kind of appraisal. A subtle up-and-down, with a slight smile teasing his perfect lips. She got the feeling he liked her wearing the things he'd bought for her and that did something weird to her insides. Like they'd taken a trip on a rollercoaster.

'The dress looks lovely,' he said as she made her way down to his level.

'You bought it, so you should know.'

The strange feelings of distance from yesterday still clung to her, even though they'd had a little reset today. A delicious coffee and pastry in a local café. A stroll through the cobbled streets where she'd picked up a few art prints as souvenirs.

'It's the wearer, not the clothing, that makes the outfit, *cara*.'

She tried to ignore the compliment, and the endearment, yet a flush of heat still crept to her cheeks. Leo had told her the dress wasn't modern couture like he'd tried to offer her before she'd put her foot down, but vintage. She'd wanted it the moment she'd set eyes on it. Glowing teal silk that had so much play of colour under the lights the dress looked alive. It was apparently from the fifties, a 'wiggle dress' the handwritten tag attached to it had said. The minute she'd slipped it on she'd fallen in love. The fit made her look like a bit of a fifties bombshell, the way it nipped in at the waist and hugged her hips.

He'd tried to imply in an offhand kind of way that being vintage, it was an economical choice and didn't offend her desire for more sustainable fashion. As if Leo didn't think she'd look up the brand on the tag. When she did, she discovered the designer was collectible and that this particular style and colour was rare, highly sought after and absurdly expensive. Yet the moment she'd placed it on her body she hadn't been able to give it up. It made her feel pretty, like she did tonight.

'You look good too. The tie's a nice touch.'

Simone wasn't unique in thinking that there was something about this man that would make even the coldest, most desiccated heart burst to life. Still, her own compliments were bland by comparison. If it bothered him, he didn't let on. All he did was stare at her. He opened his mouth and then closed it, almost hesitating. She'd never seen Leo hesitate at anything. Perhaps he thought there was something wrong with her appearance. She'd been used to criticism from her parents. Trying too hard to please them, yet never being enough.

'What?' she asked. 'Is it my hair?'

'Your hair looks effortlessly beautiful. It's perfect.'

Way to punch a woman in the solar plexus. It was like she couldn't breathe.

'I—I, thank you.'

Leo nodded. 'I have a gift for you.'

Simone clenched her jaw. Right, so that was what this was about. Would he ever stop? Each time he offered her something it was another reminder that he believed she was somehow lacking. What was it this time? Jewellery, because she didn't sparkle enough?

He'd married her, so he'd just need to get used to her as she was rather than keep trying to change her.

'We've been—'

'I know, but I thought of this dress immediately I saw them.'

He reached his hand out from behind his back and held up a pair of shoes.

They weren't just *any* shoes. These were teal patent leather stilettos which matched the colour of the dress *perfectly*. Yet what made them more striking was the flash of a red sole, contrasting magnificently with the blue green of the leather and matching the hint of red in his tie.

Red is the colour of harlots, Simone.

Her mother's words shot into her consciousness. Even after all this time, those old censures returned like a tainted muscle memory. Worse now since she'd married Leo because everyone thought of him as a god who deserved a goddess, not a mere mortal like her.

'I have perfectly good shoes.' She looked down. Hers were nice. Elegant, neutral pumps that went with everything.

Leo followed her gaze, slowly, like he was taking her all in.

'You do. However, these…'

He held them up and wiggled his hand as if that would tempt her. Simone's eyes caught the pristine red of the sole again. The man was like the serpent dangling a shiny apple in front of her. Punishingly handsome and all temptation, just like she'd expect the devil to be.

Leo might be able to get away with pretending that the dress he'd given her was just some old thing that cost nothing, rather than a coveted collector's item. He couldn't with these shoes. She knew exactly how much they'd cost. Whilst they were a drop in Leo's ocean of money, they represented a life she didn't have or want any more.

And yet the way they gleamed under the lights. They'd look *gorgeous* with what she was wearing. Those towering heels would make her much taller...

'No.'

'If you're afraid of wearing heels this high, there's no need. I won't let you stumble.'

She'd been used to high heels once. They weren't practical to her life after she'd taken up the role as an executive assistant, running around after billionaires who wanted her at their beck and call. Yet his refusal to put those tempting, magnificent shoes away caused a swirl of irritation to spark up inside.

'We've talked about this. I don't need expensive gifts. *Especially* not clothes. I'm not you.'

'Thank God for that,' he said. 'Yet there's something I know. You want them. I can see it in your eyes.'

She *hated* that he could and how right he was. She *did* want them. Wanted to put them on with their gorgeous red soles, slick on some red lipstick even though she didn't own any and to hell with the words of her mother in her head, even after all these years.

She loathed that conflict inside of her, sensations and

memories she'd thought were long buried. That fire of irritation lit to the hot burn of something a lot like anger.

Leo held out the shoes. 'It's not as if they're a choker of diamonds. They're shoes. Why say no when you know you want them?'

'Fine,' she said. He'd won. She placed her clutch on the stairs behind her. Balancing against the handrail, taking off one pump and dropping it with a thud, then another. He didn't hand her the shoes, instead, Leo stepped forwards and placed them on the floor in front of her. For a moment she had the strange sensation he was bowing down to her and the rush was intoxicating like a shot of the hazelnut liqueur she enjoyed. It was sweet and went straight to her head.

She slipped her feet into the heels, took a moment to adjust. The way they felt, her calves bunching. The height they gave her. Red be damned. She didn't care. She wanted them and she'd wear the hell out of them, even if it was only for tonight.

Leo's vibrant, knowing eyes flared with something like satisfaction.

The heels brought her to the same level as his mouth. His lips were sculpted, with a perfectly defined cupid's bow. His lower lip slightly fuller, giving him a sensual, almost brooding expression that the world loved. Right now, they tilted at the corners, carrying the hint of a smug smile. That he'd won? That she'd capitulated? Probably. She hated how she'd given in, but even more, how much she loved how the shoes looked and felt. How Leo knew.

And even with that complex conglomerate of emotions swirling inside, she longed to grab him by the tie, kiss him and wipe that devastatingly handsome smirk from his face. She took the tiniest of steps back as her fingers itched to simply reach out and take.

'Great,' she said. 'Are you happy now?'

'Very. Do you need—?'

'I don't need help. It's not like I've never worn heels before. Let's go.'

She grabbed her bag then turned in a rush at the top of the stairs, wanting to escape the craving that had over-taken her, which was turning her into someone she didn't recognise any more. How Leo made her feel. How she felt like she'd sold out when Leo was right. They were only shoes, so why did it even matter?

Then her heel caught. She pitched forward. There was a shout, she flew, then...

Morbidity. Mortality. They were both words Leo had heard when Simone had been rushed by ambulance, un-conscious, to Milan's top hospital two weeks earlier.

That moment where she'd pitched forwards, tumbled and all he'd been left with at the end was a body at the base of the stairs. The blood. Even now the vision, run-ning through his head as if it were a horror movie, jolted him like a current of electricity. Making his heart race. Twisting his gut. He *saw* Simone but imagined at the same time, his mother on a dark set of stairs, alone.

In both cases, the fall had been his fault. With his mother, for not making sure she had enough money so she wouldn't have had to work nights, cleaning. She could have taken something easier, been safe at home instead of slipping on some stairs in the cold darkness. With Simone, giving her a wretched pair of shoes she hadn't wanted. In the end, the gift more for his sake than hers, because he'd wanted to show her off, crush the moniker of *Plain Jane* for ever. In the end, he hadn't done what he'd promised her he would. He hadn't protected her from stumbling.

Instead of a dinner he'd been looking forward to with a beautiful woman, wearing what he'd bought for her, he'd been plunged into a nightmare of his own making.

The memories were stark. Her lying in bed. Her eyes closed. The side of her face florid with dark bruising. And as he looked at her, willing her to keep breathing and begging her, *Open your eyes, Simone. Please…* The image was overlaid with one of his mother. Similarly unconscious, though with all the pleading in the world, she'd never opened her eyes again.

Fortunately, that hadn't been the case for Simone. When she'd finally woken in critical care, confused and disorientated, he'd thanked the heavens for what he saw as a second chance even as the terror had gripped him. At first, she'd not been able to remember much, till the pieces of her life seemed to fall back into place like a jigsaw. The only thing she couldn't recall was what had happened in the final moment at the top of the stairs, which he took as a blessing. He wished he was similarly afflicted and could forget the vision of her stumbling, flailing, falling.

'Only a few more tests, Mrs Zanetti.'

'Thank you Doctor,' she murmured.

Leo leaned forwards in an armchair in Simone's hospital room, where he'd spent most hours every day since she'd been moved here from critical care after her fall. He checked his phone. His driver reported the paparazzi were still parked outside the hospital as they had been ever since news had broken of Simone's accident. The speculation about what had happened that night, salacious, until his lawyers had threated legal action and Simone had finally been able to issue a media statement. Or at least, his PR had issued the statement with her approval.

Thanking the hospital. Thanking Leo.

That last thanks was entirely undeserved.

He rubbed at the rough stubble on his chin, from going days without shaving, as the doctor asked her some more questions and performed yet more tests. Asked Simone to smell things, to look at charts. Neurological and other examinations all designed to test her mental status. The final steps before she was discharged.

'How is your dizziness? Photophobia?'

The blinds of her private room were closed, the lights dimmed, so Leo didn't need to hear her answer confirming she was still a little sensitive to light. He hadn't considered himself a religious man, yet the fact Simone was sitting upright in a chair and able to see at all was like every prayer he'd cast to the universe had been answered. She'd been given back to him, when his mother had been committed to a grave, in darkness for ever.

'Thank you for your care of my wife. Of us both.' His words choked in his throat. He breathed through the burn at the back of his nose. Staff had been immeasurably professional and kind, especially when for a while they'd feared her condition was critical, till scans had proved her head injury wasn't as serious as it might have been.

'You're doing well,' the specialist said. 'My star patient. We can discharge you today. I'll arrange for staff to bring the necessary paperwork and book a follow up appointment.'

As the doctor made to leave, Leo stood, held out his hand. She'd been recommended as one of Italy's finest neurosurgeons and nothing he could say to her would be enough to encompass how he felt in this moment.

'I'd like to make a donation,' he said. Money was all he had to atone for his sins. Just as it was for the people he'd harmed as a reckless teenager in Rome, it wasn't enough, but it would have to do. 'To the hospital foundation. Or is there a charity you'd prefer?'

'That's generous, Signor Zanetti. We have a foundation that evaluates novel brain injury treatment. However, there's never enough funding.'

'There will be now,' he vowed. 'I'll have my office contact you for details.'

'*Grazie*,' she said and left the room.

He walked towards Simone, sitting in a chair wearing a soft, casual black dress from her wardrobe, with gold sneakers. Items she'd asked him to bring for her. It had seemed strangely intrusive, searching through her clothes, yet as he did so, he'd gleaned a bit more about her style. How some of the things she owned that he'd never seen before, seemed a little whimsical. He wondered when she wore them. A soft and silky scarf in cornflower blue, black and orange. Earrings with little dangling enamel lemons. Things he'd never imagined she might wear yet once he'd seen them, he somehow couldn't imagine her not.

'How are you feeling?' he asked, touching Simone's hand, which was reassuringly alive with warmth. The last time he'd touched his mother her hand had begun to cool. He shuddered.

Simone looked down at his hand over hers. She shrugged. 'Fine, all things considered.'

Simone didn't look it. Her skin was pale and she had dark shadows under her eyes. She'd said that people kept waking her up through the night, every night, asking her questions and checking her vitals.

'Good. Photographers are still at the front door. Our car will be coming around back to avoid them.'

'Photographers? That's ridiculous.'

'I agree.' He knew what they wanted. To take photographs of any bruising that remained on her face and down her arm where she'd fallen. She was so lucky not to have broken anything. The marks were already fading and were at the stage of green and yellow now. They'd been gone within two weeks he'd been told. But it was still an awful reminder that things could have been so much worse. There'd been warnings about the effects of a head injury, given her period of unconsciousness and post traumatic confusion. Irritability, disinhibition, tiredness and so many more. Simone had seemed lucky to have been spared most of them. Not everyone would have been.

'Can you imagine what they'd say of me now? They wouldn't be as charitable as calling me Plain Jane.'

The heat that rose to his gut was instant and volcanic.

'Anything they say about your appearance, other than you are a beautiful woman still recovering from a serious injury, would be unwarranted and they will be punished.'

Her eyes widened. 'How would you punish them?'

It had been another failing of his. He'd believed that

most of the uncharitable commentary about Simone's appearance was an aberration that would die down if they simply ignored it long enough. No longer.

'I'll stop providing information or access to those who don't co-operate.'

His press releases were usually distributed equitably. Now, he'd cut off anyone who persisted in writing negatively about her. Circolo's media department wouldn't be happy, but he didn't give a damn.

A knock sounded at the door and it opened. An orderly walked in with a wheelchair.

'Is this necessary?' Simone asked. 'I *can* walk.'

A nurse followed behind carrying some papers. 'Since you've had dizziness, *si*. It's policy. Just to be sure.'

Simone nodded then stopped. Shut her eyes and pinched the bridge of her nose. She looked in pain and it was yet another reminder that he hadn't looked after her when he should have. When he'd promised to. After a few moments she raised her head.

'Did you manage to bring my sunglasses?'

He reached into the pocket of his jacket and pulled out a pair he'd found. He handed them to her and she slipped them on. They covered most of the visible bruising. She took a deep breath, as if steeling herself, then looked around the room.

'Okay,' she said. 'I'm ready. Let's get out of here.'

CHAPTER FIVE

THEY'D MANAGED TO avoid the photographers parked outside the hospital with a bit of subterfuge, for which Simone was thankful. She'd hated looking at herself in the mirror and at her bruises, which were still too tender to hide under makeup. There was no way she wanted photographs of herself plastered all over the press looking like this. Simone reached up and gingerly touched the back of her head. Apparently when she'd fallen, the claw clip had broken and cut into her. At the hospital they'd tried to wash the blood out as best they could, but she was told they'd had to cut away some of her hair to check her wounds. She almost didn't want to know how it looked. In the days after her injury she hadn't cared, because everything was fuzzy and terrifying when people kept asking her the year, who she was and what had happened to her. Especially that, because even now, the fall itself still remained a total blank in her memory.

'Are you all right?' Leo asked, frowning. 'Is your head sore?'

'I don't think I want to know what's happened to my hair. It feels like chunks are missing and I haven't really washed it in two weeks.'

'When you feel up to it, would you like me to organise a hairdresser to come and cut it for you?'

Something soft and warm lit in her chest. 'That'd be lovely.'

'I'll ask Marchesa to find someone suitable.'

Leo had been her only constant in the days after her fall. All she knew was that every time she woke from a sleep, Leo was reclining in a chair in her room, or sleeping on a trundle bed brought in for him because he refused to leave her side. Then the memories came back and the little bits she couldn't remember, he'd gently filled in for her. They'd been going out to dinner but she'd tripped in those beautiful high heels he'd gifted her and fallen down the stairs.

'I'm sorry about dinner with the Tessitores.'

He made a noise, an exhalation, almost like he'd been punched.

'You have nothing to be sorry for,' he said. The words spitting out of him with a surprising vehemence. 'My concerns were not about them. Only you.'

'Still—'

'There's nothing more to be said. They sent their regards and flowers, which I would have brought to you except they weren't allowed in critical care. By the time you were on the ward, they were past their best.'

A buzzing sound rang in her ears. She put her fingers to her temples. *Critical care…*

It was hard to believe how close she'd come to not being here at all.

The warmth of a hand settled on her knee, the weight of it giving her some comfort even if Leo had no idea what was troubling her.

'We're almost home.'

Their driver manoeuvred down a back street approaching a high stone wall. An automatic door opened to the underground garage of Leo's Milan residence and the car pulled to a stop. She took off her sunglasses and made a move to open the door.

'Wait here,' Leo said. He left the car and moved around to her side. He opened her door and held out his hand.

Simone shook her head. 'I'm fine, Leo. They wouldn't have released me if I wasn't.'

His expression appeared pained but he gave her what she could have described as an attempt at a warm and understanding smile. 'Humour me.'

She placed her hand in his. His touch solid. Safe. Yet nothing about Leo Zanetti was safe. The heat of that commonplace connection building through the act, simple yet powerful. She wanted to snatch her hand away but that would seem irrational, so she ignored the sensation and let him help her from the car.

'Thank you,' she said, expecting Leo to release her. He didn't and she found she didn't mind at all.

'I've cleared my study on the ground floor to make a bedroom for you there.'

'Why on earth did you do that? I don't want to move. I like the room you gave me.'

She loved the space. It was private and relaxing. One of the things she was most looking forward to after leaving the hospital was sleeping in her magnificent four poster bed, in the room Leo had designed especially for her.

He let out a slow, almost long-suffering breath.

'I thought you might say that.' Then in one swift moved he simply bent, lifted her into his arms and held her secure against his strong, hard body.

She squeaked. 'What do you think you're doing?'

He began to move, striding through the underground garage to a flight of stairs. 'I would have thought it self-evident. I'm carrying you inside the house.'

Simone wriggled in his arms. 'I don't need this. Put me down!'

Leo simply held on tighter. He made his way up the stairs as if carrying her was no effort at all. 'You've been dizzy. You left the hospital in a wheelchair. There are three flights of stairs to the upper floor where your room is. My aim is to get you there safely.'

'This is ridiculous. I was only in a wheelchair for the hospital's legal liability. I can walk on my own. I'm sure you won't let me stumble.'

Leo reached to top of the stairs, stopped. Stared at her intently. His eyes were so transfixing, hypnotically so. In this moment she developed an acute understanding of the idea that you could simply fall into a gaze and drown in it.

'Yet I didn't prevent you from stumbling and falling, and you were injured. That will *never* happen again.' His voice was deep and raw. It carried such gravitas behind it, a rough sound that seemed sincerely meant. This was important to him, her safety. Instead of feeling claustrophobic and strange as it did only minutes before, she relaxed into his embrace.

He was strong, solid. The intoxicating scent of his aftershave achingly familiar, carrying a mystery and depth that suited Leo to perfection. It was a smell she wanted to wrap herself in. To simply take whatever Leo was prepared to give.

For so long she'd been alone, with only herself to rely on. By design, because the people she was supposed to be able to trust the most, her friends, her family and the man she'd loved, had all abandoned her. This, someone wanting to look after her, seemed completely foreign. And right now she was tired of relying on herself. Tired of everything, really. She just wanted to settle in a comfortable bed of her own and sleep for a year, then wake up feeling like someone new.

After a third flight of stairs, where he didn't even break a sweat or get out of breath, Leo finally reached the door of her room. 'Are you okay for me to put you down?'

She nodded. This close it was clear how truly flawless he was. His warm, tanned skin without a single blemish. No part of him anything other than perfect. Then there was his strength. The way he moved, as if she weighed nothing at all. His hardness to her soft. He gently placed her feet on the ground and supported her, she assumed till he could make sure she was steady.

At least it didn't make her world spin, so maybe things would improve faster than she'd expected.

'Is there anything I can get you?'

'I'd love a coffee.'

'That can be arranged,' he said with a warm smile, opening the door of her room. 'You sit down. I'll be back soon.'

She walked inside the attic space and noticed immediately how much darker it was. The filmy sheers had been covered by thicker, blackout curtains. Tears prickled at her eyes and she wiped them away. He knew about her photophobia. Again, it was something Leo had done for her.

She put her sunglasses on a side table and flopped onto the soft, overstuffed couch. The neutrals of the room soothing on her overworked brain. She leaned her head back, and shut her eyes. Sifting through her memories of the wedding, Lake Garda, the waterfall, until she hit the blankness of the last few moments on the night she fell.

Nothing.

Or maybe something… There was a prickle of sensation. She opened her eyes. Leo stood at the door of her room with a tray, looking awfully domesticated.

'I thought you were asleep,' he said, walking in and setting the tray with two cups and a little bowl down on the occasional table in front of her. The rich, toasted aroma of coffee filled the room.

'Not yet. I'm trying memories out for size.'

Leo handed her a cup. Placed the little bowl in front of her, which she now saw contained some hazelnut pralines.

He sat down next to her and took a cup of his own. 'Did any fit?'

'No. My actual accident's still a blank.'

'Perhaps that's a good thing,' Leo said. 'It's not something you should want to remember.'

'I hate having moments of my life missing, even if it's only a few.' It reminded her of how fragile she was, how arbitrary life could be. 'Though I guess everyone has something they'd like to forget.'

'Indeed.'

The look on Leo's face seemed stark. Haunted. It suggested what he might have seen. From the moment she'd woken it appeared to her like he was looking at a woman returned from the dead. In the fortnight she'd been in hospital, once her shocked brain had started thinking a little more clearly, she'd begun to realise how close she might have come.

Simone didn't know what to say to make any of it better. Instead, she grabbed a chocolate and took a sip of her coffee.

'Thank you, Leo... I—'

He held up his hand in a stop motion. 'I don't want any thanks. There's nothing you have to say. If you need anything, call me and I'll come. But for now, rest. I'll see you later.'

He picked up his own coffee and stood. Striding out of the room as if being chased by a ghost, before closing the door gently behind him.

The next week passed in a blur. Given their honeymoon had been cancelled, Leo had started working again. Not going into the office but working from home. A somewhat remote yet powerful presence, as he gave Simone her space. Whilst recovering, she hadn't realised how much sleep she'd need, or how much even the little things took out of her. They'd taken a quiet walk to the local café since she was getting cabin fever and she'd slept for half a day afterwards. Her doctor had reassured her on the follow up visit that it was completely normal and she was doing remarkably well, even though her head felt like it was stuffed full of oatmeal when she woke up each morning.

All she wanted was to feel like herself again. At least her hair had been washed and styled, which helped. She was pleased with how it looked in a new below the shoulder bob. Quite a bit shorter because of how medical staff had cut into it but she could still wear it up if she wanted, which she took as a small win in what felt like weeks of losses.

She went to the bathroom and dabbed on some concealer, hiding the worst of her remaining bruises. She still looked pale and tired. Nothing a little cream blush wouldn't fix so she put some of that on too. After satisfying herself that she looked a bit more human again, Simone walked to her lounger and flopped into it, grabbing her phone. She hadn't had much communication with Circolo. Marchesa had sent her a text asking if she was okay and telling her everything was under control. Leo had shielded her from all talk of work, saying he didn't want her to worry about anything, which of course made her worry about *everything*.

Simone wanted to feel as though things were getting back to some kind of normalcy, so she opened her calendar. Checked on what she'd missed in those hazy few days when she'd woken, terrified, briefly not knowing where she was or even *who* she was till she heard Leo's voice and it came trickling back.

Her diary was absent any of Leo's appointments, which was strange because his diary was usually back-to-back. Had he cancelled everything because of her fall? It seemed shocking to her that he might have when in her experience, his business was *everything* to him. She went into his diary and it was all there. Meetings, the charity ball they were meant to attend. It must have been a glitch. Yet toggling back to hers…zero.

She flicked to her emails then, squinting and turning

down the brightness of her phone's screen. Taking it slow as she scrolled because the movement of the screen still made her feel a bit woozy. Marchesa had done a great job of clearing out most of the admin emails. There wasn't much that hadn't already been read and attended to. She glimpsed an all-company email from Leo personally, about admin support. Opened and read it.

What. The. Hell.

She gripped her phone hard. He was excluding her? Marchesa was—

Simone stood in a rush. Probably too much of a rush, her head pounding. It didn't matter. She stormed to the door of her room and flung it back, marching down the stairs to Leo's level. Stalking to the top of the stairs that would take her down to the living area. As she reached the landing, a flash of something streaked through her, like a sense of déjà vu, her heart pounding against her ribcage. Simone stopped, took a deep breath. Grabbed the railing and as much as she wanted to run down the staircase in righteous anger, she composed herself and walked slowly, carefully, till she reached the bottom.

Even though she'd taken a moment, it didn't dampen the sensation scorching and furious, surging through her veins. He wouldn't be in his study. He'd turned that into a downstairs bedroom for her, which hadn't yet been changed back after she'd refused it. *Ha!* She'd thought his offer sweet but he was yet someone else in her life who was intent on making decisions for her with no consultation. The other place she knew he appeared to enjoy was a beautiful terrace off the lounge area that led to the garden, where you could sit at a large table under a pergola covered with grape vines.

'Leo!'

The sound of a chair scraping back on sandstone tiles grated through her head. The tap, tap, tap of leather soled shoes came closer as Leo jogged into view, his brow furrowed in worry.

Well, he *should* be concerned.

'*Cara*, there's a problem?'

She pinched the bridge of her nose, the pounding of her heart starting a corresponding pounding in her head.

'You need painkillers? A doctor?'

She looked up at him. 'No, Leo. I need you to tell me why you sent an all-company email telling everyone that Marchesa's now your EA.'

He cocked his head, but didn't look at all chastened. If anything, his frown deepened.

'What are you doing looking at your email? Your doctor said you shouldn't be working—'

'She said I could have a graduated return starting one day a week and increasing as I felt fit enough. I feel fit now. What I didn't expect, was that my employer would just…just…sack me!'

Leo held up his hands. 'Husband.'

'What? You're pulling the husband card *now?*'

'*Simone.*'

That tone in his voice. She was sure Leo meant it to sound placating but instead, he sounded so condescending it made her grind her teeth.

'There's no need for you to work. I can give you everything you need. You've trained Marchesa well and she'll be able to do the job admirably.'

'There's only one problem, *husband* dearest.' She

lifted her hand, stabbing her fingers into her sternum as if punctuating every word. 'You. Didn't. Ask. *Me.*'

'I didn't want you to be concerned about anything. This seemed like a good solution—'

'As an interim measure. Nothing in our deal said I wouldn't continue in my role as your EA.'

'Circumstances change and I don't understand why—'

She began to pace, trying to expel the furious energy that had overtaken her. Leo could never understand what it was like, being subject to the whims of others. She'd *fought* to be able to make her own decisions and now he was intent on stealing everything away from her. She'd be entirely reliant on him. And when he decided he didn't want her any more... What then?

'We have an agreement, but I will not be kept. Since my twenties, I've been employed. I've *studied* to hone my skills as an EA and I'm damned good at my role. Now, you're taking it all away from me!'

She'd had enough people ruling her life, particularly her parents. Using their money as a weapon to be wielded. She'd left the family when she'd realised they'd never see her as autonomous, only as a chess piece to be moved. Where love was conditional, so long as you fit the family mould.

When she'd walked away Simone had made a promise to herself. She'd *never* go back to a situation where she wasn't in charge of her own destiny. Sure, she might be married to Leo, but she'd gone into that with her eyes *wide* open to help Holly. She'd been fooled into thinking that he'd begun to care about her, even if only a little, when what he really wanted, was to run her life how he saw fit.

'Come, sit down,' Leo said.

Her stomach twisted into agonizing knots. 'I don't need to sit down. I need you to *fix* this.'

'Simone, you look like if you don't sit down, you're going to fall down. Please.'

He moved towards her slowly as though he was approaching a wild animal. Leo touched her elbow gently. A sensation shivered through her, liquid and warm. Too pleasant and comforting. She hated that she felt like this. That he was *right*, because the emotion of it all had taken it out of her. She felt like she was wilting like a flower in baking sunshine. Knees a little unsteady. Exhausted, like all her batteries had run empty.

'Do I have to pick you up again and put you on the sofa?'

For a fleeting second a flare of heat rocketed right through her. The memory of how it felt to be in his arms. How solid. How safe. How cared for.

Yet he didn't care. If he had, he wouldn't have done this.

She needed to wrestle back the momentum. 'Fine, let's sit down then.'

Simone walked to the couch and lowered herself onto it. It was deep and as comfortable as the one in her bedroom. The moment she sank into it she decided she was never going to leave. She wanted to curl up and sleep the week away.

Leo sat next to her. Close enough, but the gulf between them seemed unbreachable.

'No one visited you at the hospital.'

Her heart rate spiked, sending another pounding into

her head. She touched her temple. Why was he bringing that up?

'I asked for your emergency contacts from HR. Called Holly. She said she couldn't come because she's pregnant and doctors won't allow her to travel. Insisted I get in touch with your parents. Gave me their details. Your father emailed me in response to keep him appraised, *should I be so inclined.*'

Simone knew he'd been in touch with Holly. The moment Simone had been well enough she'd contacted her sister to reassure her that she was fine because she didn't want Holly to worry any more than she had already. It was bad for her blood pressure. They'd exchanged messages since, Simone downplaying the aftereffects of her fall.

Holly hadn't said anything about Leo contacting their parents.

'I told you I was estranged from them.'

Leo's eyes tightened. The expression was one that looked a lot like concern but she was used to that being wrapped up in a desire to control. She wasn't buying into it, not any more.

'You were injured. Seriously. If it weren't for me, who would have cared for you?'

It was as if the world stopped. She gripped onto the arm of the sofa because that terrible truth slammed into her so suddenly. She really had no one. Work was her life. She didn't have many close friends because those she'd thought she was close to once, had laughed at her behind her back. She was caring for Holly, not the other way round. Her throat tightened. What if she'd been alone, and fallen down a flight of stairs with no one to find her? She might not be here right now.

Simone shook her head. What was she thinking? Her New York studio had only been one level. There were no stairs to fall down there. She was jumping at shadows, at possibilities that would never have arisen.

It still didn't take away the creeping, terrifying thought that she could have died when she'd barely even lived. It was like a terrible weight of realisation pressing on her chest, making it hard to breathe.

'I take care of myself. That's what most people do. You don't get to make decisions for my life.'

Everything about this, how she'd thought he cared, seemed changed. Like when she'd arrived at this house and he'd shown her to her beautiful room. Or taken her to Lake Garda to see a magnificent waterfall and garden that few people ever would. Then when she'd woken in hospital to find him by her bedside. Those fond memories curdled in her stomach like sour milk.

'I was trying to help so you didn't need to worry.'

'And yet here I am, more worried than before.' She pinched the bridge of her nose. Trying to hold back the burn in her eyes.

Leo reached out and took her hand gently. Rubbed his thumb over the back of it. Anyone looking at them might see this as a tender moment.

Looks could be *so* deceiving.

'What do you need?' he asked.

She looked at him. His expression seemed so open, concerned. She wanted to believe what her brain told her she was seeing. That he really did care. That this was an aberration and he was just trying to do the right thing, not run her life. But trust was a hard-won thing and she'd been here before. People wanting to steer her life because they didn't like the way she drove it herself.

'My job back. To ease into things as I feel ready. But you can't exclude me from making decisions. Not ever again. I though you respected my autonomy.'

Now she was scared he didn't respect anything at all.

CHAPTER SIX

In the days since their argument over Simone's work, they'd reached a form of truce. Leo was sensible enough to realise he'd overstepped, even though what he'd done was for Simone's benefit. He'd called Marchesa and apologised, saying that Simone would resume her role at her own pace, with as much or as little assistance as she chose.

All Simone's assistant had said was, *I knew she wouldn't let you go that easily.*

Simone had also demanded that he reinstate her attendance at the charity ball this evening. Whilst he'd said nothing to her, he was worried. He didn't want to stretch her too thin. Her photophobia had dissipated and she wasn't getting dizzy any more, but she still tired more easily than usual. Guilt plagued him about what he'd asked of her. It was unrelenting. The memory of Simone lying at the bottom of the stairs played over and over in his head. Yet she'd been firm, so he'd been sensible. Choosing not to pick a fight that didn't need to be fought, since clearly this was one he'd never win.

He adjusted his bow tie and checked his watch. An alert pinged on his phone, telling him their driver was on the way. He strolled from his room and waited outside. Not wanting to leave until he could safely escort Simone down the stairs.

She'd been somewhat elusive in the past week. Working with him on the days that she wanted to but otherwise taking herself into the city on her own. He'd resorted to asking Marchesa who claimed it was *secret women's business* and said nothing else. It piqued his interest but he didn't ask because he didn't want to interfere. He'd made too many mistakes already and he refused to make another, not where Simone was concerned.

She needed to understand that he valued her. To try to repair the damage he'd already inflicted.

The door of her room opened and she walked out, standing on the landing at the top of the stairs to her attic suite. At this first glimpse of her his heart simply tumbled from his chest and fell at his feet.

If there was ever a goddess embodied on earth, it was Simone in this moment. In a silk dress, encrusted with crystals, shimmering gold like sunlight at dusk. The front plunged in a vee, showing off her creamy cleavage. Draped over her shoulders and flowing down her back was a short cape, glittering with beading. The fabric clung to her curves, gleaming in the soft light.

He didn't know where to look or what to do. The heat of immediate and unrelenting desire scorched through him. Thank God his jacket was buttoned closed because her shocking effect on him would have been immediate otherwise. He'd been plunged into the ninth circle of unrequited hell.

She was so regal, like a queen greeting her subjects. Her lips the red of arterial blood. Her fingernails and toes a matching colour. On her feet she wore heels. Glittering sandals to match the dress. Tall. Spiked. He wanted to open his mouth and say something about her choice of footwear, but he gritted his teeth. She was a grown woman, as she'd already made clear. He had no right to butt into her life. That was not the relationship they had.

Yet for one brutal, blinding moment, he wished it was. He wanted to have it all.

'Exquisite,' he said. The word left his mouth before he could think. How dare anyone have ever called her plain? How could he have even dignified the idea with his own attempts at press releases to explain the way she looked when she was perfect, just the way she was?

She began to walk down the stairs. He held his breath, watching every step. Not relaxing until she was safely next to him.

'Our car's arrived,' he said hoarsely. 'Are you ready to leave?'

'Of course. I'm looking forward to it.'

Simone was a beauty with no compare. He'd known it to some extent before, but to his shame, it was as though tonight she'd been reborn and he was seeing her for the first time. He didn't know what had brought about this change but he liked it, far too much.

'Then let's go.' He held out his arm. She hesitated before slipping hers through it. They had another flight of stairs to navigate and he couldn't bear the vision now flickering through his head, of her pitching forward and falling.

She gripped the railing with one hand and lightly held his arm with the other. At the top of the stairs, his heart began to beat a rapid and thready rhythm. He made his way down slowly, one step, then another till they reached the bottom and he escorted her into the car. Safe.

'Where did you get the dress?' he asked. She glittered in the car, like the most precious of jewels he wanted to lock in a safety deposit and hide away. The sensation was overwhelming, irrational. 'I had no idea you were looking.'

She shrugged. 'It was time and Marchesa found the place for me.'

She'd put every other woman to shame tonight. There was no one who'd eclipse her. He wanted to cancel the evening. Tell the driver to turn the car around, take Simone home, carry her to the bedroom and make love to her for hours.

He hadn't been like this since he was eighteen and overfull with hormones. It had to stop. Simone had been clear about the parameters of their relationship. He was her employer. She was his executive assistant. Nothing had changed.

And until he could get himself under control, he needed distance.

'I have some people I need to speak with tonight,' he said. Business was something he could hide behind, something she'd understand. 'But I'll be claiming a dance.'

His mouth would *not* stay quiet but the temptation with her was too great. Later, after he'd taken some time, he'd be composed and back to his normal self. Then he'd dance with her, and not before.

'I'd like that,' she murmured. 'And I'll hold you to it.'

Leo was a man who kept his promises. This was one he might regret ever having made.

Their car slowed, pulling up along the red carpet of a charity ball to support homeless services. One of many similar charities that he backed after his time on the streets, in the hope of helping other young people stay out of trouble. Leo also knew that the night was a perfect one to show solidarity between Simone and himself. To put an end to whatever gossip remained in the aftermath of her fall. Still, he couldn't help thinking the night was centred on him, when all he wanted was for the focus to be on her.

The car door opened. He got out, waiting by the door as Simone left the vehicle, stepping out as if she was made of molten gold. The cries of photographers filled the night, calling their names to get their attention. He might have been used to this, ready to smile on cue, but Simone wasn't. Leo knew how intimidating a red carpet could be for the uninitiated.

He slipped his hand around her waist, almost expecting her to be stiff and uncomfortable, but she relaxed into him, as if this was where she was always meant to be. The perfect fit, just as on the night of their wedding. He leaned down, murmured in her ear.

'Just smile,' he said.

At every call of her name, Simone turned and beamed like the consummate professional she was. More beautiful than any human had a right to be. They passed through the gauntlet, talking to a few people on the way in till they got inside and he reluctantly relinquished her.

It was for the best, because whilst he wanted to keep her close, Leo knew in the end, he always had to let her go.

The ballroom was Italy at its most opulent. Frescoes adorned the ceiling. A beautiful blue sky filled with cherubs, angels and pastoral scenes. The walls gilded in an extravagant Rococo style. Chandeliers dripping from the ceiling. Huge urns of flowers filled niches along the walls. It felt as if Simone had stepped into another world, half-expecting Titania, Queen of the Fairies, to burst through a doorway at any moment.

It was glorious in its excess. Once she might have criticised it as unnecessary and frivolous but tonight, she leaned right in. The ball was for a good cause. One close to Leo's heart. She knew how much these kinds of functions could raise, when the wealthy opened their pockets. If it helped homeless teenagers like Leo had once been, all the better.

When they'd arrived, Leo had spoken to a number of people who'd all sought him out. Spending so much time in his presence, she'd noticed that people flocked to him like moths to a bright light. He was blinding.

Yet whilst he might turn every head in a space, when she'd stood at the top of the stairs outside her bedroom he'd called her…

Exquisite.

She'd liked that that's what he thought of her, perhaps a little too much, even though she shouldn't. Especially since she'd gone out on an unfamiliar limb and opted for glamour, from a small local designer. To hell with thinking the glorious, golden dress she wore was frivolous. She loved it, the way it draped and glittered. She was tired of making herself small. It was like, after her fall, this was her second chance at life and she was taking it. She'd decided she could be true to herself and still show her feminine side.

The side that still loved beautiful things.

Leo had excused himself a little earlier. Business always came first for him and she assumed he was networking about the Tessitore deal. She picked her way through the crowd of people in dinner suits and gowns and sparkling jewellery, looking for him. Once, she'd thought she didn't fit in these spaces any more but now she realised her place was wherever she wanted it to be. She didn't know where Leo was in the throng of people but she didn't take long to find him, in amongst a small group of men. Hoteliers, property magnates. Potential clients no doubt. She realised then, that Leo was moving puzzle pieces around in a way that would advantage him. Making introductions. Helping others so that they might help him right back, when he called in the favour.

She felt a burn in her belly. Was she just another puzzle piece too? Although why should she care if she was? Did she even want the answers to those questions? Simone hesitated. Maybe she could come back later...

No.

If that's what this was, she refused to allow herself to be a part of Leo's complicated jigsaw, not any more. They were supposed to be a team. She began cutting through the crowd towards him. As she approached the group, he was engrossed in conversation but some others noticed her. She wasn't a fool, she knew those looks on their faces. Admiration, attraction. Maybe it made her throw her shoulders back a little more, put a smile on her face. It was the first time in such a long time she'd felt noticed.

Simone realised she liked it. A strange tightness gripped in her chest. She'd like it a lot more if it had come from Leo rather than some strangers. At that discovery, she almost turned around and left. But he must have seen their attention move to somewhere other than him. Noticed their appraising gazes. And he turned to face her, eyebrow raised.

What was he thinking in this moment? It was hard to tell. She realised he was a man who kept a great deal hidden and whilst she might have let that slide once, now she seemed to want all of the answers.

'*Tesoro*,' he said. The endearment washed over her. It was for show and perhaps to stake a claim of sorts. 'You need something?'

Dinner was over, the band had started in earnest. She knew what she wanted…

'I was going to claim the dance you promised.'

'I'm in the middle of something right now.' He nodded to the men with him. 'I'll find you shortly.'

Was he putting her in her place? She wasn't sure, though clearly he was signifying their importance over her, because where were all their wives? Were they off in some corner somewhere, all wondering whether their husbands would ever ask them to dance too?

'Of course,' she said, not wanting to rock the boat. She wasn't sure what this discussion was about, its importance, so she didn't want to crash some business deal by being difficult. 'I'll look forward to it.'

Simone was about to leave, when Leo smiled. It didn't reach his eyes. It was the smile she'd seen him give to countless numbers of people who he'd dismissed, who were unimportant to him. A smile that was a meaningless platitude. Something exploded inside of her, a vol-

canic type of sensation that burned from her solar plexus
outwards. She gritted her teeth.

She was not going to keep herself in hiding, not any
more.

She turned with as much composure as she could, then
stalked off back through the crowd, not knowing where
she was really headed. Her usually cool, calm demeanour shattered. There was a terrace she could go to, she
supposed. Maybe she could grab a glass of champagne
and cool off, when all she wanted to do was run raging
into the night. Simone looked for a waiter as she neared
the dance floor. The couples on it all swaying to the beat
of a song designed for a slow dance.

'*Signora Zanetti.*'

The voice made her stop, a familiar one she'd heard
before, once, when after a number of approaches from
recruiters and third parties, he'd called her personally to
offer her a job. She turned and looked up at the imposing form of Rocco Silvestri.

'Mr Silvestri.'

'Rocco, please.'

Rocco and his father's company made some of the
finest and most sought-after designer furniture in the
whole of Italy. Yet Leo refused to use any of it in his
work. Anyone who worked in Circolo knew of Leo's disdain, if not enmity, for the Silvestris. She'd never asked
why as it hadn't been relevant to her role. She'd thought
it might have been that Leo and Rocco were the same
age and both were eligible, Italian bachelors. Perhaps
natural rivalry had morphed into something more than
mere competitiveness. Style magazines often compared
the two men, even though there was no comparison to be

had. In her opinion, Leo won in all ways. Though Leo didn't seem like the kind of person who'd hold a grudge for frivolous reasons. It had to be something more…

A question for another day.

'Let's not stand on formality. Call me Simone.'

The corner of Rocco's mouth kicked up. He wore a tuxedo like Leo, but was somehow stockier, brawnier. More like a fighter, as opposed to Leo's indefinable, almost aristocratic sophistication, which she realised now she preferred. Rocco was still a handsome man in his own right though, with his dark hair and dark eyes. Typical Italian good looks, she might have said. Simone could see why he always appeared to have a different woman on his arm. Although tonight he was without the usual female accompaniment.

'Your husband wouldn't like that.'

'My husband isn't here to express any thoughts on the subject.'

'Which makes me a lucky man. Where were you going in such a hurry?'

A loaded question, she was sure. Did it mean he'd been watching her? The burn might still be in her gut at Leo's rejection but she wasn't one to air her grievances in public. Especially not with someone who Leo viewed as a kind of enemy. She was angry, not petty.

'I was about to find myself a drink, whilst waiting for Leo to join me.'

'Why don't I find one for you?' Rocco made a minute gesture with his hand, and a waiter arrived like magic. She took a glass of champagne from the man's tray with thanks and sipped the chilled bubbles. Rocco took a dark, blood-coloured glass of red wine for himself.

'If I were your husband, I wouldn't be leaving you alone like this. You never know who you might run into.'

She laughed, seeing this for what it was, a kind of harmless flirtation. Probably begun by Rocco to annoy Leo.

'I'm sure I'm safe enough.'

'I'm gratified by your confidence. And why is Zanetti keeping you waiting?'

The hair prickled at the back of her neck in warning. 'Oh, you know. Business.'

Rocco lifted the glass of red to his lips, took a hefty swig. 'When there's so much pleasure to be had? What a waste.'

The band struck up another tune. This one jauntier, less romantic. She looked over at the couples there, smiling, having fun.

When was the last time she'd done the same? As Rocco had said, it seemed like such a waste. Especially this existence of work and little else. She could have fallen down a flight of stairs and never regained consciousness, and what would she have achieved out of life? Simone wasn't sure she liked the answer.

'You want to dance.'

It wasn't a question. She hated that she was so transparent.

'Yes. But I'm sure my husband will be along soon.'

Rocco snorted. Clearly not believing her. 'Why not dance with me?'

'You still have a glass of wine to drink.'

'What's a glass of wine when I can dance with a beautiful woman?'

'Now you're trying to flatter me.'

'I'm telling the truth. You'd know that if your husband told you often enough.'

If they had that sort of marriage, Rocco might be right. Still, they were admissions she couldn't make.

She raised her eyebrows. 'Perhaps it means more coming from him.'

Rocco smacked his palm to his chest as if she'd shot him through the heart. Then he started laughing. Warm, genuine and if she wasn't mistaken, a little chastened.

'I'm wounded, Signora Zanetti. And it's only a dance.'

She wasn't so sure about that, but right now, she didn't much care. Anyhow, she'd dealt with a hundred men like Rocco Silvestri before. She could do it again.

'Then it would be my pleasure.'

Rocco reached out and Simone handed him her glass. He found another waiter and deposited both on their tray and came back to her. Then he crooked his arm.

'Shall we?'

She slipped her arm through his as he led her to the dance floor. The couples there made way for them. Some looking on in interest. Most, absorbed only in each other. As they moved into the crowd, he eased one hand round her waist, took hers in the other. She placed her free hand on his shoulder, the fabric of his suit, cool under her palm. Rocco didn't try to pull her closer than he should for two strangers, keeping a respectable distance. The music's rhythm singing through her as they began to move, even though this didn't feel as seamless as it had with Leo on their wedding day. Like a shoe that was a bit too small. Like it wasn't quite the right fit.

But she wasn't looking for the right fit with Rocco Silvestri, she was just looking for fun. To find the woman she'd lost so long ago, through her family's rejection, the hard work she'd had to put in to break away, to earn her own money. She'd lost part of herself in trying to make something of her life so she could support herself, and now, support her sister. It was time to rediscover who Simone Taylor really was.

Except she wasn't Simone Taylor any more, she was Simone Zanetti. Her marriage yet another thing she'd done not for herself, but because of circumstance.

When would it ever be time just for her?

'I'm glad you appear well. Are you fully recovered from your accident?'

'I am, thank you.' Things were mostly back to normal. She still woke up a little fuzzy, and needed more sleep than normal, but she was almost back to her old self.

'Everyone appears to be watching us,' Rocco said, breaking Simone out of her reverie.

'Really?' After so long trying to fly under the radar she enjoyed hearing that perhaps, she might be creating a bit of a stir. Sure, marrying Leo had done that too, but the aftermath had been so tightly controlled by marketing, she'd felt like a chess piece being pushed around rather than a person in charge of their own destiny. Rocco guided her as they executed a seamless turn and Simone smiled. 'Surely they have enough to do rather than to worry about us?'

'The Zanetti and Silvestri rivalry is renowned.'

'And why is that?'

It seemed as reasonable to ask one of the participants in that rivalry now, as anyone else. A look passed across Rocco's face, something intense, although she saw him pull it back in. Try to hide it.

'Zanetti's a pretender. Pushing in where he wasn't invited and isn't wanted.'

Simone stiffened and the burn of indignation rose inside her. Leo might have been relatively new to the game of design after exploding onto the scene when he'd left modelling, but he'd been phenomenally successful. Nobody could deny that.

'Please don't forget, Mr Silvestri, that you're talking about my husband.'

'Your husband... *Mi dispiace*.' Whilst he might have said it, Rocco didn't seem sorry at all. 'Then why isn't he here dancing with you, instead of me?'

She opened her mouth to say something else in Leo's defence, but no words came out. She'd spent most of her life trying to fit in with what other people had wanted of her. Even when she'd broken free, her role as an executive assistant had her taking charge of other people's lives, making them easier, sometimes at the expense of her own. Then in choosing to marry Leo, it was to help Holly, not because she'd wanted it for herself.

When would *she* start to matter to others, even a little?

'So, Simone. When are you coming to work for me?' Rocco asked with a sly kind of grin teasing the corner of his lips.

She wasn't unhappy about the change of subject.

'Is that what this is about? Some kind of job interview? Why didn't you just pick up the phone?'

'I tried that once and you rejected me.'

She cocked her head. She'd told him before she was under a restraint of trade. Seemed he wasn't keen on listening. 'So you thought you'd dazzle me with your winning personality by insulting my husband?'

Rocco laughed without affectation. Like the one before, it was warm and sounded like he was genuinely amused.

'I like you, Simone. You're wasted where you are.'

She didn't have time to disagree.

Over his shoulder, into her startled vision, came Leo. Stalking through the dancers like a shark parting a school of fish. Leo's vibrant eyes fixed on her with the cool intensity of a predator watching its prey. Goosebumps showered over her skin as he approached and clapped a hand on Rocco's shoulder. Not hard enough to start a fight, but firm enough to send a message. Simone had only accepted that people were watching her and Rocco dance before. Now, she sensed the attention of the crowd shift onto the three of them.

'I'm cutting in, Silvestri.'

Rocco shrugged Leo off and turned.

'The music's not finished.'

'But your dance is.'

Rocco's grip didn't tighten, but he didn't relinquish her either.

Leo's jaw was clenched hard, his nostrils flaring. His anger appeared barely reined in. Simone wasn't sure what the issue was between them, but she wasn't about to let them have a fight over her, as perplexing and in so many ways, thrilling as that might have seemed.

No one had ever fought over her before. People were generally only too happy to give her away.

'You haven't asked the lady what she wants,' Rocco said coolly. She supposed she should have liked that he was giving the choice entirely to her but she realised it was less about her as a woman and more about needling

Leo. Intimating that Rocco cared what she thought and Leo didn't.

'*Tesoro*?'

Leo held out his hand. She took it. If there was a side to be taken here, Leo would always win.

'It seems my husband's finished what he was doing, Mr Silvestri. Thank you for the dance.'

The corner of Rocco's mouth curled in a sardonic kind of smile. 'You're not someone who required babysitting. *Alla prossima,* Simone.'

He nodded and then disappeared into the crowd without looking back.

Leo bundled her into his arms and held her close against him. Not the distance of strangers but of intimates, even though there hadn't been any intimacy between them. Every part of him seemed tight, barely leashed. Part of her liked to believe that it might have been jealousy but that would have required a certain level of emotion between them, when she knew there was none.

'There will be no *next time* with him. There shouldn't have been a *this time*,' he hissed into her ear.

The music took on an intensity. More of a tango type of beat. Leo led the dance in a way that left Simone in no doubt as to who he thought was in charge. Well, as they said, it took two to tango and she wasn't about to play whatever game he'd started. She refused to be scolded like some errant schoolgirl.

'Don't pull the jealous husband act, Leo.' He'd danced them deeper into the crowd of people on the floor, out of the way of those who'd witnessed the exchange between the two men and towards the opposite edge of the dance floor near a set of doors. Then he pushed one open and led her from the room into a darkened corridor, wheeling round to face her. Toe to toe. She didn't care. She wouldn't back down.

'If anyone could be said to have an enemy, Silvestri is mine. How do you think it looks if my *wife's* dancing with him?'

'Perhaps it looks like there's a *détente* between you.'

'*Never.* He's after my secrets. He's after my wife. What a coup that would be.'

'A coup?' she snorted. 'I wonder what the press would say about your Plain Jane wife then?'

Leo snaked his arm round her. He was so strong, so hard and uncompromising. The planes of him pressing into her, leaving no space between them, just their bodies flush against each other. Still, she had no doubt that if she demanded distance he'd give it to her.

She didn't want any distance.

'Silvestri can see what you can't. A beautiful woman,' Leo bit out. 'And you'll never have anything more to do with him.'

Simone ran hot and cold, a mix of anger and something far more potent coursing through her.

'You're not the boss of me, Leonardo Zanetti.'

His hand flexed on the small of her back, burning and possessive. 'I believe you'll find I am. You, in fact, demanded to remain in your role.'

'And what are you going to do? Terminate my services like you tried to do earlier? Be careful what you wish for. I've had more than one job offer whilst working for you. It wouldn't be hard to find another.'

'*Silvestri,*' he said, jaw clenched, clearly guessing at

least some of what she and Rocco had been discussing on the dance floor. 'There's no world in which I'd ever permit you to work for him, as your employment contract clearly sets out.'

'And that ends if you sack me rather than me leaving of my own accord. You promised me a dance, then dismissed me like I was nobody when to the world, I'm your *wife*. Well, I discovered almost dying has a way of changing your perspective on everything. I want to dance the dance. I want to live my life. *Mine*, not someone else's. I'm tired of waiting. For you, for anyone and I'm not going to do it any more. I'm done.'

She placed her hands on his chest intent on pushing him away yet instead her hands simply rested there, relishing the feel of his sculpted muscles under the fine cotton of his shirt far too much.

'You don't want to dance.'

'Oh really?' Simone asked, her heart punching at her ribs. 'Then what do I want, Leo?'

'*This*.'

His lips crashed to hers and he groaned. His mouth hard, uncompromising. The music in the background faded to nothing but white noise roaring in her ears. This was a possession, him staking a claim, and she claimed him right back.

His arms wrapped round her as a cool wall hit her back. She curled her fingers against his chest, not caring that her fingernails pricked his flesh through the fabric of his shirt. He groaned, his hands flexing and gripping her body, as if he was warring with himself when there was nothing to win here. She was already lost to him. His body pressed hard into hers. The scent of him overwhelming her, a rich, heady spice, like she'd been transported to another place. He invaded every part of her. Their mouths clashed, fused together. His tongue conquering hers, only urging her to take more, kiss harder. She was nothing but passion and flames. Perfect heat. Desire and wanting. It was dizzying. If Leo hadn't been holding her up she'd have dissolved, slipping through his grip and pooling at his feet.

He tore his mouth away, his chest heaving. The front of his shirt impossibly crushed. Now it was her turn to groan, though hers wasn't a sound of passion, but protest. She didn't want him to stop. She wanted this to never end. He took her hand in his uncompromising grip and began walking. She followed, not caring where he was leading her. He tested one door, then another, till he found one unlocked. A room in darkness, only the lights of the city illuminating it through the plate glass window. A smaller ballroom? A meeting room perhaps?

It didn't matter where, it just mattered that they were alone. He backed her into a table. His eyes glittering in the reflected city light, as he lifted her onto the surface. She wanted to be closer, melded to him. Her legs parted to accommodate his hips, and his mouth dropped to hers once more. Capturing her lips with his own. Their tongues duelling as if neither could get enough. She *burned* for him. Every part of her pure fire. The need like a living thing, ravaging through her. He rucked up her dress, his hands hot and fevered against her skin. She moaned at the feel of his palms, stroking her thighs. Then Leo placed his hands on her backside and pulled her towards him, the table height perfect. The centre of her against his hardness. He reached to her left breast, stroked a thumb over her nipple and it was like shooting stars streaking through the night sky in her head.

'What you do to me,' he murmured and flexed his hips. Simone moaned again. Wrapping her legs round his, as an ache bloomed deep inside. An empty sensation that only he could sate.

'Shhh. I told you I knew what you needed. I'll give it to you.'

He held her close, continuing to flex in a slow, steady rhythm as she rubbed herself against him, his arousal. The sleek, fine wool of his dinner suit almost rough against the over sensitised skin of her inner thighs. She craved having nothing between them. No underwear, no clothes. A bed and the two of them together naked and entwined. Yet at the same time she wouldn't give up this moment, here, in a darkened room, if someone had offered her millions.

Their breaths came in pants, like a love song to the darkness. He pulled back a little and she clutched onto his jacket, to stop him. 'More,' she said. Unable to express how much she needed him in this moment.

'It's what I'm about to give you, *cara*.'

He gently pressed his thumb against her lips and she opened as he slid it into her mouth. She sucked, running her tongue over the rough, warm flesh. Now it was his turn to moan and the power of that sound, of what she was doing to him, coursed through her like a shot of spirits.

'Minx,' he murmured, as he slipped his thumb out, tracing his hand down the front of her body, to her underwear, moving it aside and easing his thumb through her folds. She gasped, the consuming pleasure of it blooming inside her as he touched and teased. She *knew* he was toying with her, never going quite where she needed him. Perhaps he wanted her to beg him and she knew that she would, if he'd just tip her over the knife edge she skated. Then his thumb gave the merest of brushes over her clitoris, and that light touch almost caused her to burst with the force of an explosion.

'Oh, God,' she whispered. Wanting, needing.

'You called?' Leo chuckled, a dark, satisfied sound. Yet he didn't withhold much longer. Moving his thumb to the perfect spot. The centre of sensation. Stroking and circling as she was lost to him. Inside of her coiling tighter and tighter till she cracked in two. Leo captured her cries with his lips as she exploded into a million pieces, which seemed to hang and float in the room before those parts reshaped and reformed. Whole again, yet totally changed. She rested her cheek against his chest as he held her there, like she was something precious.

'We're getting a room. I want to spend the night making you scream.'

'Yes.' One word was all she was capable of uttering.

'Stay here.' Leo eased himself away for her, cupping her cheek. Gently kissing her lips. Then he buttoned his jacket and turned, stalking to the door of the room. As he opened the door, backlit against the soft light outside, he made an imposing and impressive silhouette. Looking up and down the corridor, for what, she wasn't sure. Then someone in uniform, a staff member, approached him.

'Tell your concierge it's Leonardo Zanetti,' he said, his voice deep and dark like black velvet. 'I want a room for the night. My wife's unwell.'

'Of course sir, would you also like us to call a doctor?'

'No, a room will do. We'll be waiting here.'

There was a little more hushed conversation and Leo returned. Wrapping his arms round her once more. Kissing her soft and deep. She placed her hands on his chest. The strong, solid muscles there keeping her grounded as the rest of her trembled with wanting.

'You'll be the death of me,' he murmured.

'I hope not before the night is over,' she said, running her fingers over the studs of Leo's dress shirt in an attempt at a tease. 'You have promises to keep.'

'And I will.' His voice was almost a growl. A warning. Her experience was so limited. What would it be like to be with a man like Leo? All confidence and power. Well placed arrogance and ego.

Another wave of heat flooded over her. She wanted to simply melt onto the tabletop and slide to the floor. It was as if every bone in her body, every muscle and sinew, had forgotten how to hold her up.

Within minutes, another staff member arrived. A man in a suit. The concierge she presumed.

'Signor and Signora Zanetti? I have a suite organised for you if you'd like to come with me. We can take the staff lift for privacy.'

'Thank you,' she said. Feeling a little guilty at the deception and the work it must have taken to organise a room so quickly.

They headed out and then down another corridor. Leo kept his arm possessively round her waist. The effects of her orgasm still singing through her veins, making her weak at the knees, her bones like rubber. They approached a lift at the end. The concierge activated it with a keycard and then handed something similar to Leo.

'This will take you direct to your floor. Your room's the only suite on it. You have late checkout.'

The door slid open and the man activated the button for the top floor.

'Please call us if there's anything we can do. I hope you're feeling better soon, Signora Zanetti.'

He nodded as the doors closed. Leo turned to face her, pressing her back against the lift's cool, metal wall. He cupped his hands to her jaw, thumbs gently stroking her cheek as he kissed her. Simone's lips opening under the tease of his tongue against her own. The heat. The need. All the seductive slickness of it, twisting and tightening the desire inside of her. Ramping up the sensation till she became a bright, pinpoint of wanting. In what seemed like seconds, the doors opened on their floor. Leo pulled away, cheeks slashed with a flush of colour under the burnished gold of his skin. He took her hand, led her to the door, unlocked it, then swung her as if weightless into his arms. Pushing through the door, he entered the room. A few lamps were illuminated in the opulent space but it wasn't the décor that interested her. She couldn't take her eyes from Leo's face. How intent he was. Driven. All because of her.

Goosebumps flowered over her skin, the ache deep inside intensifying again. It had been so many years since she'd made love to anyone and that was really only youthful fumbling when she'd kidded herself she was in love. Right now, she might as well have been a virgin. This was different. Leo was a man, one with a reputation and who routinely topped the best of everything lists.

It hit her with a flash of realisation. She deserved nothing less.

He strode through the space with purpose till he found the bedroom. The bed turned down for them already. He gently placed her on the carpet and held her steady when she swayed into him, a look of smug satisfaction on his face. She couldn't blame him. It was well deserved.

'Turn,' he said. His voice low and rough. She shivered at the erotic promise of the sound as she turned her back to him. An indefinable sensation like water trickling down her spine told her he was close. Then his breath caressed the back of her neck in warm gusts. After a few moments there was a touch at the base of her neck, gently stroking down to her zip. A slight tug and the cool air of the room eased the burn of her overheated flesh. After the zip was undone, Leo traced his finger gently up her spine, then swept her dress from her shoulders, as it slid down her body in a silky rush and pooled on the floor at her feet.

CHAPTER SEVEN

LEO ROCKED BACK on his heels. It was as if time had suddenly stopped. Simone stood before him in her underwear of sleek coffee-coloured satin and lace. A vision before him. The swell of her backside, the tempting nip of her waist. Her skin like rich cream. Needing to stay away but wanting to get closer.

He knew he'd put her off on the pretext of business when she'd come to find him. When she'd asked him to dance, what he wouldn't have given to simply take her hand and lead her to the dance floor. Yet he'd been trying to wrestle his aching need for her under control. This magnificent, confounding woman. That was until he'd overheard someone saying gleefully, *Silvestri's dancing with Zanetti's wife...*

Feeling stabbed in the gut at the thought, he'd left to find her immediately.

'Face me,' he ground out, words almost impossible. She inflamed him. Undid him. He wasn't a violent man though some from his past might beg to differ, yet seeing her dancing with his half-brother made him want to roar and tear apart the world. How he'd maintained any semblance of self-control in that moment, was beyond him. Leo knew why Silvestri had done it. Just another game, trying to steal something from a Zanetti that wasn't his. Leo wouldn't allow it. A Silvestri would never steal something from a Zanetti, ever again.

For as long as his ring was on her finger, Simone was *his*.

Simone turned, slowly. An attempt at a tease or shyness, he couldn't tell. It could well have been both. He knew nothing about her past and whilst she'd been working for him she hadn't dated as far as he knew. She'd been focused entirely on the job and catering to his needs. The sharp, potent stab of jealousy hit him in the gut again. No matter, tonight he'd ruin her for any other man or die trying.

What a way to go.

Finally, she faced him. Simone was glorious partly dressed. A magnificent body only hinted at under her clothes. Flesh and curves. Breasts, a perfect handful. Was she a goddess sent to tempt him? Or a siren luring him to his doom? It was hard to tell. Right now, his thoughts scattered. Leo craved to kiss and taste every part of her. Whatever she was it didn't matter. He'd be worshipping her either way.

She raised her eyes to his, almost hesitant. He wanted to leave her in no doubt how beautiful she was. He unbuttoned his jacket and her gaze dropped to his groin. With that one glance an arrow of heat shot direct to the heart of him. Tearing the jacket off, he tossed the handmade garment to the floor.

He couldn't take the distance any longer. Leo stepped forwards and took her into his arms. She was still shorter than him in her heels but tall enough to be level with his mouth. The perfect position.

'*Sei bellissima.*'

Yet she was more than merely beautiful. Something about her struck a chord deep inside. The scent of her like citrus blossom. Fresh and sweet, with a bite. Full of spring promise. He tightened his grip on her and she dissolved into his embrace as he brushed her hair over her shoulder and pursed his lips, wondering where to start. With his tongue at the centre of her, his fingers embraced by her slick heat, or simply plunging himself deep inside? All of him so greedy for her, it was difficult to decide. Yet one thing kept pounding like a drumbeat in his head. Words said over and over.

Make. Her. Yours.

He raked his teeth gently over the tender flesh at the juncture of her shoulder. She trembled in his embrace. He'd promised to make her scream and she told him she'd hold him to that.

Her cries would be the sweetest of sounds.

He opened the clasp of her bra in one practiced flick of his fingers. Drawing it from her shoulders and throwing it to the floor. Her dusky nipples tightening in the cool air of the room. He stroked her left nipple with his thumb and she moaned. When she was almost mindless, writhing against him, he pinched the tight peak and she threw her head back. Crying out in pained ecstasy.

Her last orgasm had been in the dark. Now, he'd watch as the pleasure overtook her. She wasn't there yet, but her gaze was glassy, unfocused, as if she'd retreated deep inside herself. Swept away with the pleasure of his touch and nothing else.

Something darkly possessive overtook him, a pounding drumbeat deep inside. After tonight, any other man would be swept away from her memory, for ever. Replaced only by him. His lips, his hands, the memories of him inside her.

He ceased his ministrations at her breast and slipped his hands into her underwear, gripping her bottom. Stroking. Inflaming and soothing all at once. Drawing her close. Letting her know how much she affected him. She rubbed herself against his arousal as he gritted his teeth, exercising patience and restraint because he knew this wasn't enough for her and that her frustration would only ramp up her desire.

He was right. The noises she made, of pleasure, of need, were sweet music. He hooked his fingers into her panties and began to draw them down as he followed, till he was on his knees as if in worship. Leo pressed his mouth to the golden curls at the centre of her. Slipped his tongue through her folds, then slid his hands to her hips, holding her close. Gently teasing her clitoris. She speared her fingers through his hair as shudders wracked her, but if she thought he was going to let her tip over the edge this soon, she was wrong. Tonight, she'd been playing a game with him of sorts and he aimed to return the favour before giving her what she so desperately desired. Teasing and toying as she tried to press his head closer to where she needed him most, as he enjoyed the salt sweet taste of her on his tongue.

When her moans turned into sobs, he pulled away and she swayed. He stood, picked her up in his arms again and placed her on the bed where she splayed, her body flushed pink with arousal. He slid off her shoes and dropped them behind him, then he kicked off his own and removed his socks. He tore off his shirt, his trousers, till he stood there. Flagrantly aroused. Simone licked her lips. She could use that mouth with devastating effect on him later, if that was something she enjoyed. He prayed it was. Yet for now, he needed protection before he lost himself like a teenager before he was even inside of her.

Leo strode to his jacket and bent down. Reaching into the inner pocket to a card wallet, which held two precious condoms. They'd need more but in his experience a suite like this often came prepared with whatever those who booked it might require, and he suspected this was no exception. He tossed one on the bedside table, opened another and then made a show, rolling it down himself slowly whilst she watched, her pupils huge and dark. Breath coming in fevered pants.

Whilst he would have liked to continue standing there, letting her take her fill of him, he'd reached the end of his endurance. Leo crawled over her. Buried his tongue at the centre of her once more then licked up her body. The taste of her overheated skin like the finest of wines to his senses. He took one nipple in his mouth. Sucked. Laved his tongue over till it peaked, then moved to the other. Slipped a hand between her legs to test her. So slick and wet and hot it almost undid him.

'I want you, *tesoro*. I wish you knew how much.'

She arched her hips to him. 'You couldn't want me more than I want you.'

'Let's see then.'

Leo positioned himself. Notched at the centre of her, entering slowly as she moved underneath him, then with one swift thrust, buried himself deep. The pleasure of it so fast and sharp it was as if the world exploded in a shower of stars. Simone's hands gripped his shoulders, her fingernails digging into his flesh as he began to thrust. Hard, uncompromising, yet she was there with him stroke for stroke, moving her hips in time to his relentless rhythm. There was just her and him, the soft bed and sensation. He was a captive of it. Of her. Pumping his hips and driving them both on to their ultimate pleasure. He ground into her as she pressed up into him. Both of them working as one to chase each other up to a cliff edge hanging just out of reach. Then, Simone stiffened and cried out. Her body spasming around him. That's all it took to throw him over the edge too. Falling and spinning into an abyss that seemed to have no end.

Instead, it felt more like a beginning.

Simone woke to soft light filtering through the windows of the room. The heat of a body at her back. The weight of an arm round her waist. She shut her eyes again, relishing the sensation, letting the memories flood back to a night where she'd felt truly wanted. In a way, she realised now, that she'd never experienced before. Desire washed over her like a rush of hot water. Leo had made love to her for most of the night with a ferocity and need like he was on a mission to imprint himself onto her. If he'd wanted to ruin her for anyone else, she was pretty sure he had but she didn't know why that left her both elated and untroubled. In the end, she'd been reduced to a begging mess of sensation, before they'd both crashed into a dreamless sleep.

She wasn't sorry about any of it, although she couldn't help wondering… Had he not seen her dancing with Rocco, would it have been the same? Did Leo do it just because he really wanted her, or, like Jace, because he felt he had something to prove?

Leo's hand flexed over her belly and pulled her close. Hard against him, her back to his chest.

'I can hear you thinking,' he murmured into her hair. His voice was rough with sleep. 'If you can string together any thoughts this early in the morning, I must not have done my job well enough last night.'

And there it was, like walking from central heating into a frigid winter's wind. Because that's what this was, a job. Did Leo believe he'd done his job well? Was he congratulating himself?

'Hey, hey,' he said, releasing his hold on her and easing her onto her back. He propped himself onto his elbow and looked down at her, his eyebrows raised. 'Any regrets?'

No regrets for the passion. It wasn't like she was an innocent girl. She was an adult, making her own choices. Her regrets were for the fears.

'Why would you say that?' she asked, trying to sound nonchalant.

'Your whole body was tense and when you worry you have this little crease…' he held out his finger and stroked it gently between her eyebrows, '…right here.'

Of all the things he could have said, this was the evidence he was trying to understand her. It was an insignificant thing about her and yet he'd still noticed it.

Her mother's voice immediately rang through her head. *Stop frowning, Simone. You don't want lines that injectables won't take away. Perhaps we should end that line before it really begins?*

She'd tried to book Simone an appointment with her own plastic surgeon the next day.

Simone had been eighteen.

More power to anyone to whom that appealed. Simone didn't judge. It was every woman's right to feel good about themselves, however they wanted to. But at a time when she was still trying to find herself, growing into her gawky limbs and foreign curves, it had made her feel insecure about everything. It had taken another few years for her to stop caring, once she'd realised that how she looked and presented herself wouldn't make anyone love her any more than they were ever going to. And love could be bought, anyhow.

It was all meaningless.

'No regrets,' she said.

'Then what's troubling you?'

'Do you really care?'

The words simply blurted from her mouth, all too needy. Yet she was lying naked here, both physically and emotionally, and part of her, the one that still carried her wounds, needed to know.

Leo's eyebrows shot up. 'Why would you even think to ask that question? Of course I care.'

Simone believed him. Now, questions churned inside her. So many. Leo appeared to be an open book because there'd been so much written about him. But he'd mastered the art of disclosing only what was on the surface, whilst making people believe he'd let them into a deeper part of his soul. She saw it now. Whilst she couldn't say why, she wanted to unlock that part of him that he held on to so tightly. She asked the first thing that came into her head.

'Why the rivalry with the Silvestri family?'

It was Leo's turn to frown. She reached up her own hand and stroked at the line with her forefinger, like he'd done to her. His eyes drifted shut for a moment, then he rolled over onto his back, carrying her with him. She lay, her head on his chest, palm splayed on one of his pectoral muscles dusted with dark hair, as he held her tight. Like he was a man lost at sea, holding onto her as a life preserver.

'That's a long story.'

'We have late checkout.'

He chuckled but there was nothing happy about the sound.

'We do.' Leo's chest expanded as he took in a deep breath, blew it out. His body tensed.

'Rocco Silvestri...' Leo almost spat out the name like it was poison on his lips, '...is my half-brother.'

Simone sat up, almost wrenching from his grasp in her rush to do so. Heart pounding.

'What? But I thought you didn't know who your father was?'

'I've *always* known who my father was. I simply never acknowledged him as such and nobody ever asked.'

'And does he know who y—'

'Whilst I took my mother's name, he knows *exactly* who I am.'

She had trouble believing what she'd just heard. Everything written about Leo's life...where did the fiction end and the truth begin?

'But the story of you on the streets...'

'All true. My mother and I weren't wanted. He started

another family and left my mother destitute. Vito Silvestri is a liar, a cheat and a thief.'

Simone couldn't comprehend what she was hearing
and yet she was sure Leo spoke the truth. All of him was
so tense. His lips a thin, hard line. He wouldn't look at
her, his gaze somehow distant, lost in a past where the
memories were clearly unhappy ones. This was a secret
that he'd carried, clearly weighing on him. She wanted to
purge him of it, ease that burden somehow, if she could.

Heaven knew how her own had weighed on her.

'Does Rocco know?'

A dark look cast over Leo's face, like a thundercloud
passing over the sun.

'That name is *never* to enter our bedroom again.'

The words were a growl and she shivered at the possession threaded through them. At the suggestion that
they had a bedroom, and they'd be in it together once
more.

'Of course he knows. He *must*.'

Simone guessed what Leo said made sense, even
though she wasn't so sure what with the conversation
she'd had with the man last night. But she wasn't on the
Silvestri side, she was all on Leo's. Simone reached out
her hand, stroking the soft whorls of dark hair on his
chest.

'You want to know the story,' Leo said. It wasn't a
question. The words were almost a capitulation, although
uttered with a hardness that coloured them with a hint
of defiance. She glimpsed in that moment what a proud
man he really was.

'If you want to tell it...' She didn't say she believed

he needed someone to hear it, even though that's exactly what she thought.

He turned to look at her, his gaze boring deep. Almost to her soul.

'I'll have questions of my own for you.'

Simone had little doubt but if he was giving her some of his truths, then Leo deserved some of hers, no matter how little she might want to tell them.

'Sounds fair.'

'So magnanimous,' he said, his voice droll. 'Yet it's a simple enough story. My mother and father were furniture makers and designers. They were in business together. They weren't married, something I didn't know till much later. I believed that we were a family. That's how it seemed to me, as a child.'

'Did you get your interest in design from them?'

'From my mother.' Leo's jaw clenched. 'I liked seeing how something plain, with what appeared to have little potential, could be turned into something beautiful.'

'What happened?'

'A tale as old as time. My father had an affair with a client who was, by all accounts beautiful, but also extremely wealthy. She convinced him, or perhaps he convinced her, that he'd be better in business on his own and that she could fund it. One day, he packed up and left. Took everything. Left us destitute.'

'How old were you?'

'Seven.'

She imagined him as a little boy. Whilst no photographs existed online of him from that time, she had no doubt he would have been a beautiful child. What would it have been like for him to have had a happy life, then have it ripped away from him, without warning? For his father to simply give him up. Then she considered the mathematics of it all.

'You're thirty-five.'

'Mmm.'

'A-and…' she wouldn't mention the name, '…*he's* not that much younger.'

'The affair had been going on for some time. My father led two lives. Apparently, it took time for his lover to reach an age where money held in trust for her became unencumbered. When it did, he left.'

'I don't know what to say. He just…abandoned you.'

'I accepted that my father didn't want us.' Leo laughed darkly, a bitter sound. 'But it's worse than you could imagine. I was just seventeen and I left my mother to seek my fortune in Rome. What a fool. I was young and angry but I saw and learned a lot in my two years on the streets. Everyone there had a story. Broken families, alcohol, drugs, infidelity. It was my life and that of so many other wandering souls. Then, when I was nineteen, my mother died and I had to go back to Milan and clean out her flat. And I found…'

He turned his face away from her and she knew that this hurt him. That this was where his pain lay. Something deep and ingrained like an abscess poisoning him from the inside out.

She simply sat with him, stroking his chest, saying nothing and waiting.

'…I found furniture designs, sketches. All in my mother's hand. My father wasn't the genius behind what they made. He might have been the craftsman, but the designs themselves…' Leo turned to look at her, his gaze bleak, 'He stole them from my mother.'

The acid burned in Leo's gut. His mother had never said anything to him about his father taking her designs as his own. However, the evidence was clear. He knew his mother's writing, how she drew when she'd do little sketches for him occasionally. It was her work. He was sure of it. All the pictures of furniture, the designs his father had taken and turned into his own, had been stolen.

'Did she ever try to get them back?'

Leo shook his head. 'He left her with nothing but a child to feed.'

All he could remember was her trying to keep a roof over their heads and something on the table, meagre though it was. She'd worked herself to the bone doing so. There was no time for anything else.

'With the drawings, could you prove this?' Simone asked.

At the time he was simply a young man, angry and grieving and a solicitor had said he couldn't help, not without more proof. By then, the designs had already been trademarked and registered by his father. Later, even with all his resources, there was still nothing he could do. He'd been advised that the sketches would prove nothing in a court of law.

'Not with my mother dead. Perhaps if she'd been alive, with her word against my father's and the drawings, then maybe. But with her gone and all the money behind him, there is no proof conclusive enough. Though *I* know. He became famous by building his wealth from lies and theft.'

'And that's why you hate him,' Simone said. 'For leaving your mother. Stealing from her and leaving you.'

Leo closed his eyes not wanting to see the look of pity on Simone's face. This was the part of his story he'd divulged to no one.

'Your mom must have still been young when she passed away.'

'She was in her forties.'

'I'm sorry,' Simone said, leaning over and kissing the centre of his chest, right where his aching heart lay.

'She gave up all her dreams to keep me fed, to look after me as a child and then I left, searching for my own dreams. I should have been there for her. I should have sent more money home, so she didn't have to work so hard. Then one night when coming back to her apartment from a cleaning job in winter she slipped on ice on some stairs and she died.'

He shut his eyes, fighting the burn of tears he refused to shed. He wasn't worthy of the grief. When he'd seen Simone lying broken at the bottom of those stairs, it was like his life had flashed before his eyes. History repeating itself because he'd been thinking about himself and what he'd wanted, instead of her.

'Oh, Leo,' Simone said. 'You've carried so much grief on your own.'

'Yet here I am.'

'Here you are.'

Still, he'd carried on. For so long he'd been so angry about everything. In his teens, before he'd left for Rome, it had been because he'd wanted more than the threadbare life they'd led, the constant struggle. Then trying to assuage that anger on the streets and ending up getting involved in organised crime, which was another secret he'd managed to keep hidden from the world. He'd been trying for years to help the families he'd once hurt, although it never felt like it was enough. He had to atone for his mistakes.

Simone cupped his cheek, her expression soft and full of care. 'Are you going to do anything more with what you know?'

He didn't want to talk any more. Right now, it was as if Simone had cracked open his chest and asked him to show her his heart. Although he had to admit something about the weight of all he'd been carrying, had lifted a fraction.

He didn't deserve the respite, the relief, but he'd take it, nonetheless. Take whatever else she might offer him. Herself included. But for now, he was going to share the reason for their marriage. It wasn't merely that Tessitore was a heritage brand he wanted for himself. It was so much more.

'I'm going to buy Tessitore. The Silvestris want it, badly, and they will never get it. I'm going to take the company right from underneath them.'

CHAPTER EIGHT

SIMONE SAT ON the stone terrace at the rear of the home, shaded by grape vines, overlooking the garden. She'd wandered through the space a few times since she'd been here, through the olive and fig trees. Hidden away from the bustle of Milan. A little oasis. This morning, she sipped a coffee. The silence only punctuated by the twitter of birds. It had been two days since the charity ball and they'd barely left the bedroom since arriving home. Simone rolled her shoulders, stretched her neck, enjoying the subtle aches from their lovemaking.

Simone had known Leo was a perfectionist when she'd begun working for him. He was driven, a workaholic. Everything she'd expected from a man who'd come from nothing to own an empire. She'd just never really thought what it would be like to have all that drive and perfectionism turned onto her. A wicked slide of heat journeyed through her veins. Yes, the man was a perfectionist in the bedroom too and she'd reaped all those delicious rewards. Making love through the night, into the early morning. They'd been insatiable and perfectly attuned to each other's needs, their desires. It consumed her. And Leo too, his well-earned ego seemed to be overfed by making her scream.

It's better than music, he'd murmured into her ear the night before.

It was better than just about *anything*.

'Why are you not still in bed?'

Simone shut her eyes at the deep lilt of his voice. Right now she wanted to ditch her coffee and do just that, run to the bedroom and make love all morning, but she'd come out here for a reason and Leo had a business to run. He'd left her dozing to go and work and she'd felt guilty lying there whilst there were things plaguing him, like the so-far failed attempts to purchase the Tessitore family's textile company.

She realised now what it meant to him to acquire it, as a way of avenging his mother. And whilst she didn't really think revenge was the healthiest coping strategy, she understood him better than she ever had before. For that reason, she wanted to help.

'You were working and so was I.'

He leaned over and kissed the side of her neck. She angled her head sideways allowing him more access as he drifted her lips over her sensitive skin. Goosebumps fizzed over her, making her shiver, even in the warmth of this perfect morning. Leo stroked his hand over her arm. 'Are you cold, *tesoro*? Should I take you back to bed and warm you up?'

'*Yes*, I mean, no! You make it impossible for me to think.'

'I don't want you thinking. I want you *feeling*.'

'Leave feeling till later.' She waved at the table. 'Sit down, I have some ideas.'

Leo grinned, the look one of pure wickedness. 'So do

I. Since you're not cold, did you know that ice applied in the right way can be extremely pleasurable?'

The whole of her flushed hot. She was sure she'd gone as red as if she'd suffered a bad case of sunburn.

'Leo! Take a seat. I'm *serious*.'

'So am I,' he murmured into her ear, his breath warm as it feathered against her overheated flesh.

She sighed. 'Later then.'

He gave her neck a final kiss then drew out a seat next to her and sat. Whilst he said he'd been working, he wasn't dressed for it. All he wore were a pair of black, silk pyjama bottoms, slung low on his hips. His skin a rich gold in the morning light. The man wasn't shy in showing off his body, for good reason. She knew exactly why the talent scout had taken one look at him and contracted him almost immediately.

'You said you were working and yet here you are, feasting on me with your eyes. Maybe you could feast on me for real instead?'

She only noticed then that he had his own cup of coffee in front of him. The man was a menace to her concentration and clearly an excellent multi-tasker.

'You're still not gaining any headway with the Tessitore family?' Simone asked.

Leo raked his hand through his thick, dark hair, leaving him looking gorgeously dishevelled. 'No. They blow hot, they blow cold. Right now, they're cold.'

'Are you sure they want to sell?' Simone asked.

Leo frowned. 'That's what they claim.'

'And you've tried phone calls and meetings?'

'Every approach. Direct and indirect.'

Then there was the dinner they'd meant to go to before her fall, but neither of them would mention that. She didn't want to think about it, even though she still couldn't remember the fall itself. Yet she could see it in Leo's eyes, a distant expression. He seemed to remember it all too well. What must it have been like, to see her lying there? Especially after his mother had died after an accident like hers?

Simone couldn't imagine. Maybe that's why he'd reacted like he had. Clearing her diary and giving Marchesa her job, albeit fleetingly. He'd been trying to *protect* her, not control her.

'What are you thinking of?' Leo asked.

That she'd had a stunning realisation, but there was no time to dwell on it now.

'They're a family,' she said. 'That's why you married me. Because they had trouble with you and your play-boy lifestyle.'

'Yes. They're a deeply traditional Lombardi family, who've been textile makers for centuries. Where are we going with this?'

'Then that's what you have to show them,' Simone said patiently. 'You might have married me, but that didn't really mean anything to them. With you, it's been all about the business. You need to make it about family instead. Show them who you really are.'

Leo cocked his head. 'I'm not sure how to do that.'

She understood him a little better now. Leo held back, always kept something in reserve. He was well-liked and on the surface seemed to connect with people, but deep down, there was something about himself he protected. Spaces he kept his own. Things locked deep inside he wouldn't divulge. He was known as a consummate busi-

nessman, warm and generous with charities. Yet at their
wedding, were there any real friends of his there? Allies, yes. But did they go any deeper? She wondered if he
ever let anyone get close to him, at all. And that's what
he needed to do to gain Tessitore, if only Leo could let
it happen.

'Invite them here for dinner. To your home, not your
office, not a fine restaurant. Here, where you can host
them. It's a place you've always kept private, so why
don't you show it to the Tessitores?'

She stood with her cup of coffee in hand and began
walking around the terraced area, envisaging what she
had in mind.

'It can still be a business dinner, but something a little
more casual. Maybe out here with a long table under the
vines. It's a beautiful space if the weather's good. Maybe
I could cook something?'

Leo raised his eyebrows. 'My wife does not need to
cook. I have a personal chef.'

'Yes, yes…and he's brilliant.' Each meal magnificent,
a refrigerator always full on the days he didn't work. Details of each meal left behind, what was in it, how to heat
it up. She felt spoiled, but having a chef wasn't the same.
'But there's a soft power in real hospitality.'

At the back of the property was a vibrant kitchen garden with eggplant, tomatoes, radicchio, rucola and other
vegetables and herbs. Had Leo's chef and gardener not
protected that patch of the home as their own domain, she
would have made something with it all. Maybe in time…

She wasn't sure where that random thought was
headed.

'We can use vegetables from the kitchen garden.' She

waved to the back of the property. 'Eat—I don't know—not fine food, but something a little more homely. Traditional from the region. I could make something, but maybe not so traditionally Italian, if you think they'd like that? It can still be about business, but with a more personal touch. You've been showing them Leonardo Zanetti, the empire builder. Maybe you need to let them get a peek of Leo Zanetti, the man behind it all.'

Leo cocked his head. He was thinking about it. Simone was pretty sure that it would work. 'What would you cook?'

She thought back to her training in hospitality as a young woman and what made a good wife for a wealthy man. Whilst her parents had had a chef too, and her mother was renowned for her parties, she'd always said to Simone…

A woman should know how to mix one good cocktail, make one great hors d'oeuvre and have a signature dessert.

So Simone had learned to make a martini and smoked salmon canapes. As for dessert…

'I make a mean caramel apple pie,' she said. 'I think I'd cook one of those. That's my favourite.'

'I enjoy sweet things.'

The way Leo looked at her in this moment, with such intensity. The vivid blue of his eyes, which should seem so cold, piercing through her like a hot poker. The man could inflame with a single glance.

'So, what do you think?'

He downed the last of his coffee and stood, as if charged with a kind of fresh energy. The consummate businessman, hard, driven. Leonardo Zanetti at his best.

'Nothing I've tried has made any real headway. I'll get in touch with them. Arrange something and we'll see.' Then he looked down at her and smiled, something rare, precious and real. The type of smile Leo granted to only a privileged few. She finally felt like one of them.

'You're inspired, Simone. And I believe it might just work.'

It was an uncomfortable sensation inviting people into his Milan home, the one place in the world that he'd kept apart from everything else. Let lifestyle magazines and style bloggers wax lyrical over his other properties dotted for convenience throughout the world, the showcases to display his 'expansive vision and impeccable eye' as they liked to say. But this was the one place few strangers ever glimpsed. A private space where he could hide away and lick wounds he allowed no one else to see.

The first home he'd ever bought for himself.

Yet here, he'd shown Simone those wounds. Let her in. And now, watching her with the chef, his housekeeper, planning for this dinner, setting the table, dotting fresh flowers in empty corners, he realised that here, she *fit*. It left him feeling discombobulated, how seamlessly she had taken over his life.

Perhaps that's the way it had always been. How she'd managed his workload, suppliers, clients. Made his life simpler in every way as his executive assistant and yet he'd never truly recognised it before.

Now, the time had ticked over to eight and the doorbell rang. Simone smiled.

'I guess it's showtime,' she said, looking magnificent. Her hair in a messy updo. Wearing flared black trousers that fitted her to perfection. A white halter neck top in a silky kind of fabric, with a tracery of black and silver flowers. A bow at the back of the neck with ties trailing down her spine that his fingers itched to undo. She was the picture of sophistication, the consummate hostess. He'd underestimated her, when he should have expected nothing less.

Tonight, they had minimal staff in the home. The chef, some servers to help, but he and Simone had agreed this was to feel like a family dinner. Something more intimate, even if vitally important. They greeted the Tessitore family at the door. Patriarch, Gino and his wife, Fia, daughter, Rita, and her husband, Enzo. It seemed warm enough. Kisses for Simone, handshakes for him. Firm but not crushing in an attempt at some futile power play.

'Please,' Simone said as she led the delegation through the house. 'Come through. I thought we could have some drinks and canapes before the final touches are put to the meal.'

They entered the lounge, one of his favourite spaces here. Overlooking the garden outside, still light out being summer. The bell-shaped flowers of his mother's favourite, a Madonna Lily, nodding in the breeze.

Simone invited everyone to sit, but Rita stood in the doorway, looking at an armchair in the corner. A minimalist design of sleek, honeyed wood burnished with age. Covered with a worn and well-loved fabric he'd never changed, in a bold floral style of red, blue and gold. He'd modelled the whole room around it.

The one piece he had left from his childhood, designed by his mother. They'd had a house full once, but he suspected she'd sold it all when his father had left.

Leo should hate it, because it was likely crafted by the man, but all he saw when he looked at the piece was the beauty of its timeless design. His *mother's* design.

'Vintage Tessitore fabric,' Rita said, with a slight frown. He'd never thought to check, because he'd never recover the piece. He wondered if they thought the moment contrived, when it turned out to be a strange coincidence. Simone moved close, placing her hand on his back. He welcomed the silent support.

'I was unaware of that. It was my mother's chair. She designed furniture. That's the original fabric I recall from my childhood. I never wanted to recover it.'

'Our daughter maintains our archive,' Gino said, as he took his place next to Fia. 'We've tried to keep a sample of most fabrics the family have designed, in modern times at least. I didn't know your mother designed furniture. It looks a little like a Silvestri piece.'

Leo clenched his jaw, breathed through the heat like lava rising through his gut.

Simone rubbed her thumb over his spine, grounding him. 'My husband holds a great deal close to his chest. Family most of all. Now, would you all like a drink and some hors d'oeuvres?'

He looked down at her and smiled at the perfect save before getting the drinks as Simone offered a tray of delicacies to their guests, and sat.

'These are delicious,' Rita said.

'They're my favourite. Smoked salmon canapes. My mother always said a woman should know how to mix one good cocktail, make a great hors d'oeuvre and have a signature dessert. The hors d'oeuvres and dessert tonight, are mine.'

It was strange, her mention of family, when he knew so little of her past apart from the estrangement. He'd never asked why. That seemed like a critical failing that he needed to rectify.

'If the dessert is as good as the canape, I can't wait. I love sweet things.'

'So does my husband.' Simone laughed, casting him a knowing look that was like a punch of heat arrowing to his groin. The woman could invoke incinerating desire with a glance.

'It's comforting to see that you're recovered after your fall,' Fia said. 'We were shocked to hear the news.'

'And thank you for the flowers you sent me. It was so thoughtful. It's been difficult at times, but I'm mostly recovered. The care I received was excellent.' She looked up at Leo and smiled. 'Both from the medical professionals and from my husband.'

Gino took a sip from his drink, fixed Leo with his dark, assessing gaze. 'It must have been difficult, so soon after you were married.'

Leo knew that this night was a set of crossroads where he faced a choice, to open up to these people who were strangers to him, or remain firmly closed. Over the years many had tried to take from him, bring him down. Saying he was too much, or not enough. A pretender to the role he'd claimed and made his own, as the arbiter of all things stylish, whether they be a person or a piece of furniture. For that reason, he didn't give readily of himself about anything that would impact the image he'd spent years cultivating. The one that hid the worst side of himself. Being closed was easy.

Yet tonight was about building relationships. Showing his true self when some days, he wasn't sure who that was any more.

He glanced at Simone. She kept things hidden too and yet in so many ways, she brought out in him what was most authentic. He'd told her more about himself than he'd revealed to anyone. Not everything, that was true. There were some things in his past no one needed to know. However, it was enough to allow himself to feel a little less…constrained.

'Few know that in my late teens my mother fell after work one night and died from her injuries. Simone's fall…it brought back some terrible memories, but at least this time I was there. If I hadn't been, it could have been so much worse.'

Simone reached out her hand, placed it over his and squeezed. It was more comfort than he deserved.

'It was a silly accident, really. I put on a new pair of heels Leo had gifted me and tripped. But I'm here and everything's fine.'

Everything might not have been and that still haunted him.

'I can't imagine what that must have been like,' Rita said, looking lovingly at Enzo.

'No, yet my wife continues to wear heels,' Leo said dryly.

'I *love* heels.' Simone gave a wry laugh. 'Just not around stairs.'

His guests laughed a little too, the mood lighter. Simone turned to him with a soft smile. What she was trying to convey, he wasn't sure. The emotions inside of him too tangled to properly interpret the meaning. She knew the story of his mother, so he hadn't said anything that would have come as a surprise.

Out of the corner of his eye he glimpsed movement. One of his household staff. They discreetly signalled to Simone.

'Ah,' she said. 'Dinner's ready. Would you like to join us outside? We thought it was a beautiful night so we could eat on the patio under the vines.'

Simone joined the rest of the guests, leading them through the home. Only Gino held back to walk with Leo, looking on as his wife, daughter and son-in-law, chatted to her.

'We're alike, you and I,' Gino said. 'Lucky men. Our women are too good for us.'

Simone laughed at something said, warm and gracious.

Leo couldn't help but agree.

CHAPTER NINE

IF EMPTY PLATES were anything to go by, then Simone judged that the dinner had been a huge success. It had been a simple enough yet traditional Milanese meal. Osso Bucco, risotto, some salads made from greens grown in the garden. She'd wanted it to feel like something homely, rather than a business meal and it had worked. The patio, where they sat, was lit up with fairy lights. The vibe elegantly casual. Simone was sure that all of this was something Leo wouldn't have agreed to if asked, but she hadn't asked and he'd let her organise everything.

Considering the man controlled every facet of his life and his image, it had come as a surprise. She'd expected him to have asked the chef about the menu, or say something about the flurry of activity around the house in preparation, but he hadn't even offered any advice. It was so unlike their wedding, when he'd planned the whole thing down to the last second. Even when he'd offered her a choice, she *knew* it was under sufferance and he'd had a firm view of what he wanted.

This? It made her feel trusted. Valued. Like she had an opinion and a place in his life. It meant something.

'Your apple pie was magnificent,' Rita said. She was

about Leo's age, with short black hair and dark, expressive eyes.

'Thank you. I worried it might be a bit heavy after the meal we just had but...'

'I know. Dessert. How can you go wrong?' Rita smiled. 'It reminds me of my time studying in the US. I must have the recipe.'

'Of course. Before you go give me your email. I'll send it to you.'

There'd been some talk of business tonight. How to grow and evolve a brand. Meatier topics such as the challenges of managing a business that relied on a discretionary spend, in a downturn. Leo was less affected, the Tessitores a little more so. Is that why they'd talked of selling their business? What should have been a purely financial transaction seemed so much more. She'd always suspected that it was personal for them. She began to believe it more strongly, but there was something else. Simone wondered if they wanted to sell at all. These were questions everyone seemed to be skirting round. Something almost...personal. She guessed that it would have to be a very personal decision to divest yourself of a company that had been in your family for generations...

'May I ask...' She directed her question to Fia, who she'd discovered had been Tessitore's designer for a number of years. It was how she and Gino had met, a workplace romance. 'I understand you're looking to sell Tessitore Fabrics. But why, since you so clearly love the company? It's been in the family for generations. You're still the principal designer.'

It was like a stylus scratching across a record, as if she'd said something discordant and the sound simply stopped. If there'd been an elephant in the room, it had just stomped into plain sight. Fia gave a sad smile.

'My health.'

Gino reached out and placed his hand over his wife's, just like she'd done for Leo.

'I'm sorry for raising it,' Simone said.

Fia sighed. 'No, no. It's been a long time coming. It was a flaw that we relied too much on me and my designs. And as for our children, it's not where their talents and interests lie. Rita is an archivist. My son, a textile chemist. My granddaughter, my son's eldest, is artistic and we've encouraged her to try fabric design. She shows immense promise, but she's only fifteen and who knows what she'll want to do when she's older.'

'So there's currently no one you trust but yourself?'

Fia shook her head. 'No, we have some designers.'

'But they're not Fia,' Gino said.

Leo had sat back, watching. Not really contributing, until this moment. 'How much time are you looking at, before your health intervenes and divesting becomes a necessity?'

Fia shrugged. 'It's my eyes, a rare condition. I require surgery, though not immediately. Whilst I can still design, it's sometimes harder to do what I used to. Surgery carries risks. If it's unsuccessful my sight will deteriorate. If the risks eventuate, I'll be left unable to see. So perhaps it's time to move on, spend it with grandchildren and family and work less. You believe you're invincible, until suddenly you find out you're not. Then you have to think about life and what you need to do.'

It was all so familiar to Simone. How she still felt

about grasping what was offered to you and not letting it simply slide by. Life was for living, not merely existing.

She should know. She'd existed for long enough.

'I know that feeling, even though it's for different reasons. Life can be short. One day everything's fine. The next, everything can change in an instant.'

Everyone around the table looked sombre, nodding.

'I'm only sorry for dampening the mood of a lovely evening by asking,' Simone said.

'No.' Leo turned to her. There was something in his gaze, an intensity, like he'd been lit from within. It *burned*. Then he focussed on the Tessitores once more. 'This is an important discussion. I'm coming to understand that you're under pressure to do something. Would I be right in saying that if things were different, you wouldn't be looking to sell the company at all?'

The family members looked at each other. Gino shook his head.

'Fia is the soul of the designs. If we had more time, other plans could be put in place. If it happened in ten years, our granddaughter might have been old enough and interested enough to join the company. For now, nothing's clear and our only interest is in seeing Tessitore survive. We'd prefer to plan, than to sell when the news is out and the vultures have started circling.'

Leo lounged back in his dining chair. The space was lit up by candles and the glittering lights above them. People might like to believe he was relaxed. However, Simone knew him far better. She could see it, the way he was thinking. The merest furrow on his brow when he turned and the light catching his face the right way. Appearing relaxed yet really, just all power sheathed. Like she'd thought once before. A panther waiting to spring onto its prey. A liquid kind of heat flooded through Simone. Pooling, settling low. There was a reason no one should ever underestimate Leo Zanetti and she was witnessing it right now.

'What if I proposed not a sale or takeover, but a partnership? Circolo has the financial capacity to support the business if it needs to transition. That could give Tessitore time and space. The family wouldn't have to forgo all their shares. Should Fia have the capacity or desire, she could still design. Should your granddaughter decide her future lies with the business, and she has the talent, the opportunity to continue the family tradition wouldn't be lost to her. Then, hasty decisions wouldn't need to be made. We could invite guest designers to create fabrics whilst Fia's getting treatment. It might be a better solution for you.'

Fia and Rita's eyes widened. They smiled. Gino cocked his head and fixed Leo with a dark, assessing gaze.

'What do you get from the deal?'

Leo laughed. 'Don't worry. I'm no charity and I'll take my fair share but I understand the importance of tradition. Circolo would be partnering with the oldest and finest textile maker in Italy. That would give us significant cultural and design capital. I'd expect exclusivity on certain fabric patterns, which only Circolo branded or approved products would carry. I might ask for a veto on who the fabrics can be sold to. I can draw up terms, then we can talk more, should you be interested in my offer.'

Simone sat back in her chair. Simply marvelling as Leo had pivoted so effortlessly. But even more, he'd taken

the realisation that the family didn't want to sell and offered something which let them keep at least part of the
company in the family. They didn't have to let it go. The
offer was stunning. Generous.

It showed a new side to him she hadn't known existed.

Gino looked at his family. Fia and Rita nodded. 'Then
we might be able to make a deal.'

There seemed to be a lightness that came over the
table. A sense of hope. They drank wine, talked some
more. A friendly getting-to-know-you, till it was time for
them to leave. It was like the edge had been burnished
from the evening, sharp sides sanded smooth. Leo and
Simone walked them to the front door and said their
warm goodbyes. After closing the door, he turned. The
look on his face intent. He stalked towards her, backing
her towards the wall. Pressed her up against it, a hand
above her head.

'You are an inspiration.'

So was he, but she didn't have time to say so before
his mouth crashed onto hers. A kiss hard and fierce,
tasting like the after-dinner espresso they'd consumed.
Leo devoured her. She kissed him back, her body going
up in flames. She didn't know how she survived him
without perpetually crumbling to ashes at his feet. His
tongue danced with hers, inflaming, enticing. Whilst
kissing him was one of her life's greatest pleasures, it
wasn't enough. She needed more. She needed *everything*.
She grabbed his shirt and pulled him even closer as he
groaned. Their bodies melded together. He could take
her right here and it wouldn't matter but instead he pulled
away, his lips gleaming in the soft light, breaths coming
in heavy pants.

'I want you.'

'I need you,' she said.

The feelings he ignited inside, consumed her. A complex mix of passion, possession and completion. Feeling settled and unsettled, all at the same time.

He swooped her into his arms and captured her lips again before striding through the house and up the stairs to the main bedroom. Crossing the threshold, the only light in the room came from the ensuite, casting the space in a contrast of golden glow and shadow. For all the aggressive passion, Leo let her go gently. Placing her carefully on her feet. It was such a small thing and it still meant the world that he could think about her, when she knew he was as desperate as she was for them to be naked together. But whilst she wanted to be selfish and take, tonight she also wanted to give. He'd shared his past with people and it had been no small thing, given how deep she knew his wounds ran. How her own fall had re-opened them.

Leo toed out of his shoes, stripped off his belt as Simone began unbuttoning his shirt, tugging it from his trousers then tossing it to the floor. He undid the bow at her neck, the halter neck top falling free to her waist, exposing her breasts. He grunted as her nipples tightened in the cool air of the room. Leo cupped them with his hands, stroked his thumbs over the hard peaks.

'*Perfetto*,' he murmured. '*Amore mio, sei una bellezza.*'

Whilst she could listen to him for hours, Simone was too desperate. She wiggled away, undid her own pants, threw off her top. Stood in front of him in nothing but the fine lace and silk panties she'd chosen because she knew he loved them.

'On the bed,' she said, injecting as much dominance into her voice as she could muster. Trying to wrestle control of the evening for herself.

He cocked an eyebrow, his eyes glittering like sapphires in the light. 'Really?'

His voice was as rich and rough as coffee grounds. His fingers flexed and released as if he wanted to touch her, but she was sure that he'd like this game. Being with Leo gave her a new kind of confidence and she wanted to give him the same pleasure that he always seemed to give her.

'Yes, really. I intend to have my wicked way with you. Or doesn't the great Leo Zanetti want to listen to what he might find is actually good for him?'

Leo chuckled. '*Tesoro*, I'm happy for you to do whatever you want to me. I'm looking forward to it.'

He moved onto the bed, flopping onto the mattress in a way that suggested he was being imposed upon. Yet she knew it was an act. Leo lay there, arms behind his head, a smug smile on his face. He'd ceded control to her but she knew that he wasn't giving it away completely. She wanted to break him apart like he routinely did to her, break herself and then let them be stitched back together. Entwined, knitted. Two cracked halves making the other whole.

She eased off her panties in a slow tease, then undid his trousers and slid them from his body. Hooked her fingers into his black briefs, dragging them away and tossing them over her shoulder. A liquid heat pooled low in her belly as his impressive erection sprung free. She loved the sight of him, potent, aroused, intoxicating. Simone licked her lips.

'Want a taste of what I have?' he asked hoarsely.

'I'm hungry for you, Leo. You'd better hang on.'

He chuckled but when she took him in hand the sound was rapidly cut off. She smiled, then lowered her head and wrapped her mouth round his smooth, silk-steel length. He was salt and sweet and everything she could have desired in this moment. Simone relished teasing him with her tongue as he gripped the covers of the bed. She *ached* for him. He'd barely touched her yet and already she needed to clamp her legs together against the burn that built at her core. Could she come like this, with not a hand of his on her? Feasting on him? After so many years of feeling nothing, no desire, like walking through a kind of haze, this was a revelation.

Simone looked up at him, as his head arched back. The sounds he made, not so elegant and restrained now, but feral and out of control. She knew he was close, as his body quaked, but she didn't want the moment to end yet. Perhaps she was still allowed a little selfishness, but she wanted him inside her. She eased away from him and he groaned, his eyes glassy and distant with arousal. She crawled over his body, sliding the centre of herself over his length, relishing in his hardness, how slick they both were. Him from her mouth and her because of how Leo always affected her.

The burn built between her legs as she rubbed herself back and forth, his hands on her backside, encouraging her. She was panting now, close. So close. Simone sat up.

'Condom,' she whispered. She reached over to his bedside drawer and grabbed a foil packet. Her fingers were trembling and she fumbled so Leo took it gently from her, tore it open and slid it down his length in one practiced move. Simone leaned forwards and kissed him again, their mouths clinging to each other as she lifted herself and positioned him at her entrance. Lowering herself onto him, relishing the sensation of being filled. The relief of it so intense it was all she could do not to orgasm in that moment. He groaned and gripped his hands tight to her thighs as she took all of him in. Rising and falling as she toyed with her nipples because she knew he'd love to see her doing that. Arrows of pleasure spearing between her legs whilst she rode him. He released one of her thighs, easing his thumb between her folds to her clitoris, circling and stroking.

It was like a competition now, as to who would win and come last. The pleasure burning through her. She clenched her body around him and his breaths became shuddering gasps as he stopped lying there taking what she gave and began to thrust up into her. Simone was lost to the sensation. It was all heat and need until Leo's movements became uncoordinated and he threw his head back, shouting her name.

Words toyed at the edges of her consciousness about what this meant, what *he* meant, although they were elusive, formless things. More feeling than reality. Then the conflagration of ecstasy roared over her, burning her to the quick. Simone fell to his chest. He took her in his arms and the world became soft and hazy as Leo's coiled body relaxed and she drifted into an intoxicated sleep.

CHAPTER TEN

THE SOFT MORNING light bled through the room's curtains as Leo woke to the chirping of birds. He checked the time. Still early after their late night. Yet he didn't feel tired, he felt invigorated. A deal with the Tessitores was close. He wouldn't relax till it was final; however a partnership would be a masterstroke. He had little doubt it would be marvelled over, considered a coup of sorts. Together, he was sure they could do great things and he'd ensure that the Silvestri family never got their hands on Tessitore fabrics for their furniture, ever again. They'd have to find another supplier, someone inferior, because there was no company quite like Tessitore Textiles.

All of that had been made possible by the woman lying next to him. He propped himself up on his elbow and looked down on her sleeping form. Her hair a golden tangle on the pristine cream cotton of the pillow. Sheet round her waist. She looked peaceful in slumber, that slight line he sometimes saw between her brows when she concentrated, smoothed away. A warmth lit inside of him, a sensation intensely satisfying, like in those days on the streets when he'd been bone-numbingly hungry and had managed to make enough money for a fulfilling meal. He realised his whole adult life had been about searching for something more, interspersed with only brief moments like now, when he felt he had *enough*.

This morning, it was as if he was finally sated.

Of course, it could have simply been a hangover of their lovemaking the night before. Her lips were a revelation. Then the vision of her looking like a goddess, over him. Taking her own pleasure from his body. Giving him pleasure in return, an experience so mind blowing, it had been a struggle to hold onto consciousness long enough to scoop her into his arms before he'd tumbled into a deep, dreamless sleep.

Those memories were enough to have him hard, aching and wanting again, but there was something more. Simone was a mystery. She remained an enigma. Intelligent, beautiful, but in many ways as far away from him as the day he'd employed her. It was like a tiny splinter digging into him, an irritation.

He'd given her some of himself and yet she'd shared nothing of herself at all. He'd told her once that he'd have questions and that time was now. To him, his failure to ask anything of her now seemed like a personal one. He wanted to know what she liked, disliked. What kind of life she'd come from, why she was estranged from most of her family.

Simone was a puzzle he wanted to solve. He had questions. He could think of no better time than today for her to answer them.

As if some sense in her knew, Simone stirred. Her eyes fluttering open. At first her gaze was unfocused but then she fixed her cool grey eyes on him and the most beatific smile broke over her face, like a shaft of sunshine through a crack in the curtains. It was as if that beautiful light in her smile settled smack in the middle of his chest. An unfamiliar warmth, soft and bright. He rubbed at the spot with the heel of his palm.

'Good morning,' she said, her voice a little husky from sleep.

'It's an excellent morning.'

Simone lifted her hand and traced one gentle finger from the base of his throat to where that warmth in his chest had begun to ignite and burn. She placed her own palm over it as if somehow, deeply and intuitively, she knew it was there. Did she feel the same when she looked at him, when he smiled at her? It was yet another question in the long list he had for her.

'Last night went well I think.'

'Thanks to you.'

'All I did was to ask a question everybody seemed to want to avoid.'

'I was planning to address the issue over drinks at the end of the meal.'

A little crease formed in the centre of her brow again. He wanted to reach out and stroke it away.

'Sorry to change your game plan.'

He shook his head. 'It was perfect. *You* were perfect. From me, there would have been no way for the question not to sound forced. From you, it was organic, curious. Thank you. For that, and for your food. It made the evening far easier. I don't believe I'd have achieved the result as quickly, on my own. I've been dancing around Gino for months. I believe even had I asked outright, he would never have told me about Fia's illness.'

A flush bled across her cheeks. Simone gave a self-satisfied, and well deserved, smile.

'You're a revelation, *tesoro*.'

'I'm just me. What you see is what you get.'

'You're an enigma and a mystery. You know about me and yet I know so little about you.'

Her soft grey gaze left him, to where her left hand toyed with the sheet as if wanting to wrap it more tightly round herself. She shrugged.

'You're the interesting one. The one whose story regularly makes the press.'

'Yes, I'm a legend in my own lifetime,' he said. 'Such an achievement. Whereas you... I said that one day I'd ask questions. Today is that day.'

'So early in the morning when there are more interesting things we could be doing...'

She arched her back. Simone was in avoidance but her display wasn't contrived. Her nipples peaked in perfect, dusky points. Tight with desire. She was temptation incarnate. He could immerse himself in the pleasure of her body for hours on end and never be sated.

Yet, that didn't seem like enough. Not now. He wanted to *know* her. Not simply as his efficient, insightful personal assistant, convenient wife and now, lover. He wanted to share thoughts, *feelings*.

'Questions now, distractions later,' he said.

She pouted, but he could see the skin puckering at the side of her mouth where she was worrying the flesh with her teeth.

'Then I need coffee.'

'I'm happy to oblige you.'

Leo left the bed and as he did so he could almost feel Simone's eyes on him, as palpable as her fingers digging into skin. There were no staff in the house this early and the grounds were private so there was no need for him to dress. Leo strolled to the door of their room. If she liked what she saw, then he'd give her a show. He walked to the kitchens and set about what he'd always found to be the relaxing routine of making coffee. Espresso for him, caffè latte for her. Since she believed she needed a little fortifying he hunted through the cupboards and found some hazelnut syrup, adding a dash to her drink. He placed both cups on a tray and then carried them back to their room.

Leo couldn't imagine what Simone might have to tell him. Did she believe he'd judge her? After his own past, he was in no position to condemn anyone else, although she didn't know that. Some things, about himself at least, there was no need to disclose. Nothing she'd done would have been worse than his own youthful actions, of that he could be assured. As he walked back into the room Simone was sitting up in bed. Her hair was neater, as if she'd brushed it. She was wearing his shirt, the one torn away and discarded in passion the night before. A rush of heat flooded over him, possession, at the sight of her in a piece of his clothing. The way it swamped her. Made her look somehow small, fragile. In that moment, he didn't want to talk. He wanted to scoop her into his arms and hold her. Tell her it would all be okay, even if he didn't know what the problem was. As he came into the room her grey eyes became stormy, darkened. Not too fragile for desire then, which was good. He could work with that.

'Like what you see?'

Her gaze drifting over his naked body, fixing at his groin. In a moment he was half hard. Simone did that to him. If he didn't constantly wrestle his own desire under control when she was around, he'd never get any work done.

'A tray of coffee? Yes.'

He chuckled. If he was another kind of man, that comment might have cut him off at the knees, the way she said it. Dry as ancient dust.

'Don't prefer the look of anything else?'

'Mr Zanetti, I do believe you're fishing for compliments.' The corners of her mouth quirked as if she was trying very hard to suppress a smile.

'I don't need any, given you orgasmed into near unconsciousness last night. I feel none are required.'

She raised a slender, pale brow. 'I might suggest that you were similarly affected, but unlike you, I wouldn't like to brag.'

He chuckled, loving how Simone tried to put him in his place, even if right now it was only for show. She'd always had a way of keeping him grounded, reminding him that he was simply a man and not the ridiculously titled Sultan of Style as the press proclaimed. He placed the tray of coffee on his bedside table and propped up his own pillows. Slid under the covers and then handed Simone her coffee, taking his own and finishing it in a few short mouthfuls.

Simone looked to be savouring hers, eyes fluttering shut at the taste. Her throat dipped softly in a swallow and she took another almost as if fortifying herself. Her chest rose and fell in a deep breath, then she opened her eyes, her jaw seeming hard, as if she was somehow resolved. She placed her cup down.

'Thank you. The hazelnut was a lovely touch.'

'*Prego.* This isn't your last meal, Simone.'

She snorted. 'There are things I don't talk about much.'

'Like why nobody visited you at the hospital after your accident.'

'Holly can't travel right now, which she told you. And you know the rest of my family and I are estranged. You of all people should understand what that's like.'

'Yet I told you why. Now I'm asking the same of you.'

Simone let out a slow, pained breath. 'Let's just say there were expectations placed on me as a child and a young woman. I was supposed to look and act a certain way, to prepare myself for finding a husband my parents approved of, or even better, marrying a person they chose for me, who might help my father's business. I always guessed the idea of choice was really an illusion.'

'What sort of husband were they looking for?'

'Funnily enough, probably someone a lot like you, although not Italian. An American would have been preferred.'

'And you didn't want that.'

'No, yet here I am. The delicious irony of my situation.'

'All to help your sister.'

Simone nodded. 'You know she's pregnant. Holly hid it, till she couldn't any more. And for good reason. My parents didn't react well and threw her out of their home. Holly needed a place to live, medical care. The pregnancy's complicated and once she has the baby he'll need a stable life, a good education. I could do a lot on what I'm paid, but it didn't cover everything she needed. Now, she can have whatever she wants.'

'What about you? Your wants?'

'I wasn't looking for love. You agreed. And I was confident you wouldn't ask anything of me that I wasn't prepared to give.'

In truth, she'd given him almost everything. At least he could be confident that she'd come to his bed out of desire rather than any sense of obligation. Yet he *had* taken from her and she'd almost lost her life in the process. She'd been clear when they'd signed the pre-nuptial agreement that love wasn't on the table. In his extensive experience, most women he'd known had wanted love in the end. He'd had to be quite clear with anyone he'd spent consistent time with that whilst he'd be generous financially, and in the bedroom, love and permanence would never be on the cards. He'd been wedded to his business and that was all he'd needed.

What was her reason?

'What happened to you, *cara*? What really made you leave?'

Simone took another long sip of coffee. Sat staring at the wall ahead of her, not at him.

'When you're young, it's easy to believe a lot of things. Mine's an old, well-worn story. I was at college. I met a boy. I thought I'd fallen in love.'

She seemed to somehow shrink into herself, become smaller. He wanted to take her into his arms but she seemed so distant right now. He feared that if he did, he wouldn't get the story or the insights that he needed, to try to understand her. Maybe that was selfish of him, but Leo was also driven to find out more about her.

'He was on a partial scholarship and wasn't the sort of person that my parents would have approved of. I didn't care. He said he loved me and I thought I loved him. I had all these dreams, you know? Saving myself for marriage. Just being with one man, in love, for ever. My friends seemed supportive but really, they thought I'd lowered myself. Word got back to my parents who paid him off and the relationship ended. His professed love for me was worth a surprisingly paltry sum, in the end. I suppose he could have finished college debt free. Anyhow, he'd seen me as a conquest, a challenge, nothing more.'

She placed her coffee cup down on the bedside table and wrapped her arms round her waist in a protective move.

'My parents claimed to love me, but it was transactional. They loved us only as long as we did what they wanted. Look at me. Look at my sister. Then Jace. He said he loved me. We had dreams and promises and he didn't love me at all. Money was worth more than I ever was.'

As she spoke, Leo's heart felt like it was being crushed inside of him. Sure, he'd seen the damage misplaced romantic love could do to a person. Yet, in the end, he'd always been sure of his mother's love of him. It was one of the things that drove him, what he was doing in her name. Whilst he'd been alone for a long time, the desire to avenge what had happened to them always carried him forwards. For Simone, what did she have? Only herself. In that way she was a thousand times stronger than he was.

'You're worth—'

'I know *exactly* how much I'm worth.'

He wasn't sure whether she was talking about her intrinsic value as a person or their pre-nuptial agreement. He hated to think that all she saw her worth coming down to was a financial value of some sort. Leo cupped her cheek. She leaned her face into it, the warm weight of her in his palm. Her eyes glittering as if with unshed tears. Perhaps she wasn't as immune to it all as she pretended to be.

Even touching her, the distance between them seemed too far. He needed to close it, to comfort her in the only way he knew how.

'Come here,' he said, opening his arms. She shuffled over and into his embrace as he held her against his chest. His lips to her hair. Breathing her in.

'I'm sorry for what happened to you.'

'It was clear that the universe was teaching me some powerful lessons and I learned them well.'

Leo wrapped his arms tighter round her, to try as much as he could to let her know that she had his support, for as long as she needed it. Because whilst Simone might have believed the universe had taught her powerful lessons, he wasn't sure that what she'd learned were the right ones.

They'd had a slow start to the morning, drinking coffee together. Eating a quiet breakfast on the terrace. Something about purging herself to him, telling Leo about her past as he'd done with her, was freeing. It was like a weight lifted, one person to share her past with because even Holly hadn't really known what went on and Simone hadn't wanted to burden her. She would have been happy for a quiet day round the house, easing back into a little work except Leo had suggested he take her sightseeing and then out to dinner. Turning off their phones and forgetting about work for a while. Now, they sat in the back of a taxi, travelling to the centre of the city.

'Are you ever going to give me any hints about where we're going, other than what I should be wearing?'

Leo grinned, his eyes hidden behind dark sunglasses. He'd told her to wear clothes to cover her knees and her shoulders, and also put on comfortable shoes.

'I like surprising you,' he said. 'Although, you always seem so resistant.'

'*I* like to be prepared.'

'And yet each time we've gone out, you have been. Have I ever let you down?'

She sat with that for a while and of course the answer was clear. No, he hadn't.

'Anyway, as much as I'd like to spend every day locked in the bedroom making love to you, we had to cancel our honeymoon. I thought you might like to play tourist instead.'

Spending days in bed with him sounded like a *perfect* honeymoon. Still, Leo's suggestion was kind. Thoughtful. Something unfamiliar to her when she spent so much time thinking of others. On previous times she'd been to Milan they'd worked. One night she'd managed to get to La Scala, but that was all. It was nice to take the time to look around, especially with her own personal tour guide. The most handsome tour guide in the whole of Italy, if not the world.

'I always wondered about your choice of Verona. I thought the whole point of getting married was a happily ever after. Romeo and Juliet didn't achieve that.'

'I thought Verona was romantic.'

That gave her pause. Nothing about their marriage

was romantic and yet that's what he'd wanted for their honeymoon? She shouldn't read too much into it. A romantic honeymoon was good for PR. That had been the reason behind it, she was sure.

'It's a town famous for two hormonal kids who thought they were in love coming to a sticky end because of a family feud.'

'And yet, people find it compelling. I can't remember you being this cynical before, Mrs Zanetti.'

She hadn't been, once. Simone had been too trusting, too naïve. Believing that her life would work out well, because why shouldn't it? She'd only really recognised the privilege of the position she'd once held, when that position was taken away from her. It had taught her that in her world, people only cared about how you looked and how you dressed. That you behaved yourself and didn't create a scandal. Love was transactional. So long as you toed the line it was fine, but heaven help you wanting a little something for yourself, or trying to break out of the mould created for you, because then people didn't want you at all.

'What is it they say? *Marry in haste, repent at leisure*? Are you repenting, Leo?'

A look passed over his face. Not exactly a frown, more like a moment of something that looked like pain. Though it had disappeared so quickly she could have imagined it.

'I may have many things to repent for. Marrying you is not on the list. This will never be something I regret.'

The vehemence of his words. She didn't know what to say because the truth was, she couldn't regret this either. She was saved from having to respond as their cab pulled up at the side of a street. Leo paid with a generous tip and they both hopped out.

'It's not far,' Leo said, holding out his hand. She took it, threading her fingers through his as they began to walk. 'In fact, there it is.'

Rising above the cityscape were the spires of Milan's magnificent Duomo cathedral.

'I thought you might like to see the terraces. If there's one thing you should do in Milan, it's this.'

The plain marble square in front showed off the elaborate gothic architecture to perfection. People milled around, taking photos. A few children chased pigeons which took flight, flapping only a small distance away to land, before being chased again. They walked up to the door, avoiding the queue. Someone met them and handed Leo two tickets.

'So, we don't have to line up?'

He took off his sunglasses and winked. 'No. I have a few friends in high places. It pays to know me.'

She placed her hand on his chest. 'Why, Mr Zanetti, you do come with some benefits.'

His pupils flared dark in the languid blue of his eyes. 'Later I'll show you just how many, but for now, come explore.'

They walked inside the vast space. The floors, beautifully patterned marble. The plain walls spliced with jewel coloured stained glass windows. The vaulted ceiling, soaring above them. The cathedral's magnificence gave her a new perspective on her own existence. It made many of her all too human problems seem small, insignificant.

'We should see the terraces first, then we can explore the rest of the building, if you wish. I might light a candle…after.'

To honour his mother. She reached out and squeezed his hand. He squeezed back.

'How do we get up top?' she asked.

'There's an elevator for which we have tickets, or we can climb over two hundred stairs. Your preference?'

It sounded like the decision was hers to make and whatever she chose didn't matter, but there was a tightness around his eyes that told another story.

'Let's do the elevator.'

It was almost like he let out a long breath. 'Good choice.'

Even with their express tickets, there was a small queue. When they finally got into the lift Leo seemed bristling with what she guessed was excitement.

'This is the best view of the city. Even with all the tourists it's one of my favourite places in Milan.'

The doors opened, and they walked out through a plain, stone-walled corridor, then up a few more stairs and onto a rooftop.

Simone gasped.

Above them towered the Gothic spires of the cathedral, like a forest of stone intent on piercing the heavens. Each spire topped with a figure, like sentinels watching over the city. Everywhere she turned there was another intricate carving. Gargoyles, animals, people. The flying buttresses a marvel in themselves, richly decorated with their own architectural carvings.

'This…' Words were stolen from her. It was overwhelming, surrounded by all the glorious excess.

'Now you understand why it's my favourite place in

the city,' he said pointing. 'Look. It's clear enough. Today you can see the Alps.'

The mountains rose above the horizon, capped in snow.

'It's so beautiful.'

He smiled, but Leo's gaze wasn't on the view, but on her. 'I know.'

The moment seemed to slow, like a pause in the world turning. Then he blinked and focused on the city ahead of them.

'Would you like a photograph to send to Holly?'

'That'd be great,' she said pulling her phone out of her bag, setting up the camera and handing it to him. She stood with the spires and buttresses behind her, smiling as he took pictures.

'That should do for now.' He handed the phone back to her. She opened her gallery and flicked through. She almost couldn't recognise herself because she looked…

Happy.

As she was about to slip her phone back into her bag a text notification popped up on the screen. Whilst they were having downtime, it was from Circolo's accountant. She opened the message in case it was important.

Leo hasn't picked up.
Pls ask him to call re the charity for Roma.

Strange, she didn't know anything about Rome, or a charity.

'I have a message from Roberto. Something about Rome? He wants you to call. It sounds urgent.'

Leo's mouth tightened almost imperceptibly. 'I'll deal with it later. We're sightseeing, remember?'

'Are you sure? Is there anything—'

'No. Nothing.'

She frowned. Leo walked up to her, reached out and stroked his finger gently down the middle of her forehead, as if smoothing out the crease there.

'Allow us to have this time. If there's anything I need your help with, I'll ask. I recognise your value to me, in all things.'

He pressed her against the marble balustrade, slid his arms round her waist, dropped his head and captured her lips in a gentle, passionate kiss.

It was like she was standing on a precipice of choices and in this moment she simply let herself fall into it, above this beautiful city, like she was standing in the heavens. It overwhelmed her, the sensation.

She felt valued. She felt seen.

She felt loved.

The kisses slowed to a stop, and Leo pulled back. She looked up at him—so solid, tall, those shoulders broad enough to carry the weight of a world. To carry hers. He had a soft, knowing smile on his face. It was on the tip of her tongue, to say three words that might change them both for ever. But now wasn't the right time—not when everything was so new. Like a butterfly just hatched from its chrysalis, its wings fragile and fresh.

It needed some more time, till those wings became solid and it could take flight. So that's what she'd give it, since time was what she'd been granted. Because whilst she'd almost died, Leo had shown her a life she wanted to live.

CHAPTER ELEVEN

SIMONE WALKED INTO Leo's Milan office. They'd returned to work and she joined him a few days a week, working the rest from home. She always enjoyed coming back here. In New York, his office was high in the sky, the view an imposing one. It was as if Leo wanted to look over the city he now ruled, because he'd brought his business to the US and become an overnight sensation, rather like he had when he'd been plucked from the streets here. Yet Milan was different. The ground floor in the more historical part of town, with large plate glass windows overlooking a lush green garden accessible to staff. A lot like his Milan home, she realised. It seemed in this city, Leo was more himself than anywhere else.

Yet today, there was something edgy about him. There had been for a few weeks now, ever since their visit to the Duomo. At night, things hadn't changed. He still held her. Made love to her. Told her she was worth more than she knew and then showed her with his lips and hands. His whole body. Yet something was off. It made her ache inside, like he seemed to be drawing away when she wanted to hold onto him even tighter. To tell him that this no longer felt like a business deal. It felt real.

'I have a jet on standby for Rome, if you need it.'

He looked up at her. Distracted. Gave her a tight smile. It could be the Tessitore deal. Things had moved frighteningly fast since that dinner with the family. Long hours worked to put together something everyone was happy with. They'd sent the contract off a week earlier, which Leo had already signed, so confident he'd been that what he'd proposed would win them over. They were still waiting for an official response…

'Thank you,' he said, his eyes flicking back to his phone almost like she was an afterthought. Her stomach clenched. She couldn't help feeling as if something was wrong yet how could it be when the passion between them was undiminished? Like he could never get enough of her. It had to be Tessitore, they were so close but still so far. And yet…

'Are you sure you don't want me to come with you?'

He'd been cryptic about the possible trip to Rome but then he'd promised that if he needed her, he'd ask and she trusted him to do so. Leo frowned, and shook his head. 'No. You stay here and wait for the Tessitore contract to come through.'

It made sense on an intellectual level, but her waiting behind wasn't necessary. Someone else could open the envelope if it arrived and if there was a problem, the Tessitores or their lawyer would call. That could be done anywhere in the world. The thought of him simply going without her…they hadn't been apart since they'd been married.

Since when had she become so needy? She was a grown woman. She could spend a night away from her husband—

Except nothing was certain, nothing was real. Her

desires unvoiced. She looked at the rings on her finger. How they glittered under the lights. Still new, and
beautiful. Thoughtful, and personally designed by Leo
for her. Their marriage might not have started out being
real but it felt that way now. Her suite in Milan, a beautiful testament to his thoughtfulness, now only a place
that she kept her clothes, having moved permanently
into his bedroom.

'I just thought…'

He raised an eyebrow, his blue eyes blindingly bright
and his expression unfathomable. She didn't know what
she really thought, or how to voice this complex mess of
feelings that seemed to overtake her. Admiration, desire,
something all-encompassing and endless.

'I won't be gone long. If I need to stay it'll only be a
day or two at most.'

She opened her mouth to say something, to argue but
she wasn't sure why. Why this trip didn't feel normal,
but like distance was growing between them. There was
a quiet rap at the door. A welcome break from the ten-
sion. Simone went to see who it was and one of the staff
stood there.

'A delivery's just come through.'

The staff member handed over a large envelope. She
took it, turned it over. Saw where it had come from, her
heart skipping a beat. She held it out to Leo.

'From the Tessitores. Do you think…?'

Leo stood, his nostrils flaring. Any distance she'd
perceived, disappeared. It was replaced by bristling expectation.

'You open it. The success is as much yours as it is
mine.'

Simone carefully opened the envelope. Slid the sheaves of paper from it. A letter she didn't read being in Italian, which she was trying to learn, and the contract Circolo had returned. She flicked over to the last page.

It was signed.

She carefully placed it on the desk in front of him. This business deal had meant so much to Leo, and it had begun to take on the same importance to her as well. A spike of adrenaline coursed through her. It was done, the reason for their marriage, fulfilled...

Was that why he was pulling away, because her usefulness had ended? It wouldn't be the first time that had happened to her... No, that's not what was happening here. This was more. She knew it. Whilst it should be an ending she couldn't help but think of it as a beginning. She smiled as Leo looked at the page, traced his finger over the Tessitore signature as if he didn't quite believe it, then looked up at her. The expression on his face, fierce. He stalked out from behind the desk towards her.

'I couldn't have done this without you.'

Leo took her into his arms and her body instantly relaxed. All her worries and fears gone as he held her, then his lips crashed on to hers. She kissed him with all the emotion she'd held within herself. Thrusting her hands into his hair, gripping tight, not wanting to let him go. They were a team. Unstoppable. It was like together, anything was possible. He pressed her back against the desk and lifted her up onto it, pushing up the skirt of her dress. Stepping into her, pulling her forwards. His hardness against her core. She burned for him. It was the same as the night of the ball when he'd taken her into a darkened room and their passion had exploded for the first time. This was madness. The office door was unlocked, anyone could walk in, and yet she didn't care. He eased one hand up, toying with her nipple through her bra and she moaned softly, gripping the front of his shirt, not wanting to let go. He pulled away from the kiss, trailing his lips up her neck to her ear. Whispering words in Italian she couldn't grasp. Endearments, encouragement, thanks? She couldn't be sure and she didn't care. Then he eased his hand to her centre, teasing her body through her panties. Capturing her lips again as she moaned louder this time. So much inside wanting to simply take flight. Things that she never expected to voice again, emotions that she couldn't deny or hold in any longer as he stroked her and wound her higher and tighter. Then the orgasm simply exploded through her. Searing and hot, rolling on and on like there'd never be an end. Just like she wanted for them. But like all good things, it did end, easing, stuttering, then finally stopping. Leaving her floating in a haze of bliss and what she knew was inescapable.

They were good together. A team. Professionally, but more important, personally. Simone was certain that they were better as one than apart. And then the words she'd tried to hold in simply came out on a sigh.

'I love you, Leo.'

He was hard, aching. Wanting release. Wanting to forget. Rome had become a problem. A place he needed to travel to in order to continue to try to put to bed the sins of his past by helping the families he'd hurt. Then the Tessitore contract had arrived and he'd lost his head completely. Simone had wrecked him and remade him. But her words...

I love you, Leo.

No. That had never been part of the deal. It was based on a lie. She claimed to love him but he was a man who'd been created by the media, hiding his sins. Carefully curating his life so that he could atone for his crimes in peace.

Her words had just shattered everything he knew or wanted. He couldn't be trusted with love. He couldn't be trusted with her.

She'd slumped against him, replete, and part of him ached to simply ignore what she'd said and make love to her, here, on his desktop. But in doing that he'd be cementing the fantasy she'd wrapped herself in. One where she could truly love him for who he was, and he was actually deserving of that love.

He pushed away from her and she looked up at him, her glassy grey eyes confused.

'Do you...?' Her cheeks flushed pink. He adjusted himself, uncomfortable but that was his problem. This, between them, needed to be dealt with.

'I'm perfectly fine.'

Her face crumpled a little, before she put on what he saw now was her own carefully crafted mask. He rounded his desk and gathered up the precious contract. Read the attached letter. Soon he'd be informing the Silvestris that once their existing agreements with Tessitore had expired, they wouldn't be renewed.

It should have been a triumph. He didn't know why it suddenly felt so meaningless.

'Okay then,' Simone said, though the words were only a whisper. She began straightening her clothes. 'I might just go—'

'You can't love me.'

She turned back to him, eyes wide, skin pale, like all the life had been drained from her. A lot like when he'd first seen her lying in her hospital bed. All his fault. But he wouldn't think of that. He couldn't...

'Isn't that for me to decide?'

'That wasn't the deal.'

'Deals can change.'

'This one never will.'

He'd taken enough from her. Over the past two weeks he'd realised that's what everyone did. Her parents, her ex, even her sister Holly. She had so much to offer and now he'd done the same. Married her because she'd been perfect for his plans, not thinking how it might affect her. Making love to her when he should have known better. He'd thought only of himself and she'd almost died because of it. Simone didn't need someone like him who could never give her what she truly deserved. Who had *taken* from her without any thought. She needed someone whose heart was open. To free herself from the self-imposed shackles of her own hurt and pain and to live. To *love*.

It felt as if a switchblade had speared through his ribs.

He could never be that man, when all he'd done was take from her.

'You're a businessman. You know that's not true.'

She was so beautiful, standing there wanting and hoping. Her cheeks still flushed from the orgasm he'd given her. That she hoped for more at all, let him know he was right to push her away. He was not the man for her. In truth, he never was and never could be. Releasing her from this arrangement was a kindness, even if doing so required some cruelty.

To show her the man he really was.

'There, you're wrong. Since my teens, I've only ever cared for myself. Me and *my* needs were what was important. That's never changed.'

She shook her head. Whilst she said she'd learned lessons in life it was so like her to try to see the best, even if she was looking at the worst.

'That's not true.'

'This man you see here? He's concocted from lies. You're only seeing who you want to, Simone. Not who *I am*.'

'Then who are you? You keep yourself so closed off. If you'd just let me in—'

'You want to know me?' Leo strolled forward with the swagger he'd used in the old days when he was full of bravado and out to extort money from some small business owner. Not surprising how it came back so easily, like another part of him. An evil twin. Two sides to one coin. 'Then you need to know about Rome.'

Her eyes widened and she chewed on her bottom lip like she was afraid of what he might say. Good. Leo knew she'd wanted to come with him to that cursed city and he'd refused. He hadn't wanted her tainted by what he'd done, or finding out because he'd feared what she might think of him. Now, he wanted her to think the worst because in the end, that's all that would save her from him.

'I want to know *you*.'

He held out his arms, 'Well, here I am *cara*, ready

to tell it all. I told you I'd left home when I was barely seventeen, travelling to make my fortune. Tired of my mother and my life. Nothing was enough. I wanted *more*.'

His mother had cried when he'd left but in his bravado he hadn't really cared. He'd promised to send back money. But there wasn't much he could do as a teenager with no skills or education past high school. He'd been impoverished and homeless when the gang had found him and made him feel as though, finally, he had some worth.

'I was cold and hungry, on the streets. Too proud to return to Milan. But I found an underbelly and embraced it. A gang, who needed the type of services I could provide because I was tall and strong. But I could also be very convincing, so they hired me for a very specific task.'

Whilst he didn't want to look at Simone, to see her disgust, he couldn't help himself. Yet all he saw was her eyes filled with tears. A look of sympathy. It was wholly undeserved.

'Who you see here is a man who was happy to stand over people for money. Extorting small business owners. Feared on the streets, not caring who I ruined. I even had a nickname. One I was proud of. The Handsome Viper.'

In truth, he'd loathed the title but he'd owned it at the time because he was playing a part and instilling fear got the job done, without blood being spilled. If everyone thought him beautiful but deadly, then all the better for them. It was survival in a vicious world. He'd played a role and played it well. Just like he had when modelling. Just like he was doing now.

'I don't believe you.'

As much as Leo didn't want to, here he knew he needed to sink the knife deep.

'Then you're fooling yourself. I'm still the Handsome Viper if I want to be. I used people for my own ends, because it suited me. Just like I used you, although I admit you were paid handsomely for it. That's certainly new for me, paying money instead of taking it. Now the Tessitore deal's done, there's no need for this charade to continue any longer.'

The tears in Simone's eyes spilled over onto her cheeks. 'Don't do this to us.'

'There is no 'us', there never was. One day you'll see that I…how did you put it…*dazzled* you, just like you accused me of doing to other staff.'

She shook her head, her spine stiffening. 'No, you never fooled me. I walked into this marriage with my eyes open. I won't have you treating me like some innocent with no clue.'

'For someone who claims they weren't fooled, you're certainly acting like one, so let me be clear. By the time I get back from Rome, I want you gone. You can be out of Milan and in the US in a matter of hours. I'm sure you'd like to see your sister again.'

'So, I'm being dismissed.'

He shrugged, taking his fill of her because he knew she was about to leave. Simone's eyes were as cold and hard as flint. She'd told him she understood her worth and she wasn't going to take this lying down.

'I don't much care. There'll be a role in the company if you want it. If you choose to resign, you'll receive excellent references. You were, after all, an exceptional and most attentive executive assistant. I couldn't ask for better.'

'Thank you for making things so crystal clear. But I refuse to stay where I'm not wanted.'

She turned and strode to the door, placed her hand on the handle. Hesitated. He knew he needed to make sure she walked away with no shred of hope or love left in her.

'Oh, Simone.' He'd pitched his voice softer, ready for the final strike. She whipped round, eyes a little wide. Still looking for the best in him.

'Yes, Leo.'

'I'd like your resignation in writing, to make sure it's official. Don't forget the NDA. Or the restraint of trade that prohibits you from ever working for Rocco Silvestri. I'll enforce both to the full extent of my abilities should you choose to breach either.'

She reared back like she'd taken a direct hit. He knew they were the words that ended any chance of reconciliation. Exactly what he wanted.

'Don't worry, Mr Zanetti. I wouldn't want to experience any more of your venom.'

No matter how much of what he'd said had cut him to the marrow, it was for the best. He hoped she now hated him as much as he hated himself. It was better for her in every way.

Far better than loving him.

CHAPTER TWELVE

LEO SAT IN the bar, a bustling place, but not one of the popular tourist traps. It was a hole in the wall, frequented by locals or those in the know. He couldn't be alone, yet he didn't want to speak to anybody. Here, in the noise, surrounded by people, he could lose himself.

He took out his phone and checked Circolo's intranet for a photograph that had been posted by the team. The one of him and Simone, from Lake Garda. A moment frozen in time when he'd had something good within his grasp and simply didn't hold on tight enough. He'd let it go.

Right now, Leo had everything he believed he'd wanted and yet he had nothing at all. The Tessitore deal had been signed, sealed and delivered. Within days, a message would be sent to the Silvestri company that after their current orders had been fulfilled, they would never use Tessitore textiles again. It should have made him feel like a victor, yet he felt like a loser in all ways.

He took another slug of his drink, not caring about its quality. Cheap Grappa, because he was punishing himself with firewater. After his mother had died, he'd had so many regrets. But most of all, he wished he could have had the time back to say all the things he'd left unsaid.

Now, he wished he could have had the time over not to say some words, but to keep his mouth shut.

He'd hurt Simone. Callously. Deliberately. Leo deeply regretted the way he'd ended things, even though it had been better for her, to cut things off with no hope of reconciliation. Whilst he might always look back, he wanted her to look forwards to a life without him. To find someone to love who was good. Whose background wasn't tainted by sins of the past. She'd almost died because of him and he hadn't let her go, even then. Because he was a selfish man, who only ever thought about his own needs, and people suffered as a consequence. If Simone had stayed with him any longer, she would have suffered too.

She'd lived enough of her life for others. Running round after him as his executive assistant, marrying for Holly's sake. It was time for her to live for herself. She had money. Their agreement also stipulated a generous settlement on their divorce, so she'd never have to worry, about herself or her sister again.

It was done. She hadn't resigned yet, but it was only a matter of time before the official letter hit his inbox.

So, why did he feel so empty? He downed another mouthful of his drink, continuing the punishment he'd started an hour ago. Drowning his sorrows, yet they weren't drowning fast enough.

'You look like a man who's lost something valuable. Or someone.'

Rocco Silvestri.

Leo gripped his glass so hard he thought it might crack, but that didn't matter. The pain of broken glass might assuage his guilt.

Leo said nothing. Took another sip. The fluid burned

in his gut. Or was that anger? Perhaps the night was getting hazy, as he'd wanted it to.

'Leave now, Silvestri,' he hissed, slamming his glass on the counter.

Rocco picked it up and sniffed. 'Cheap booze. You might pretend to have left the streets but you never actually did.'

Leo turned on his seat and stood slowly. Maybe a little unsteadily. 'This boy from the streets has just bested you.'

He was sure Rocco was goading him and that no one knew what he'd done. How he'd threatened people, stood over them, destroyed livelihoods that he was still trying to rectify.

Rocco snorted. 'Bested me? You wish.'

'I have a deal with Tessitore.'

Leo should have felt satisfied at Rocco's frown, but it was like he was dead inside. Whereas once he might have taken pleasure in what was to come, there was no pleasure to be had any more. Numbness was all he sought.

'You're speaking rubbish.'

'You wish,' Leo echoed because he could be petty too. 'I now have an exclusive partnership with them. As long as that exists, your furniture will never use another metre of Tessitore fabric in any design.'

'I see you're trying to bring them down to your level rather than elevate them.' Rocco said with a sneer. 'Since you seem to be making new acquisitions, maybe I'll make some of my own.'

'I don't care what you acquire. You're wasting your time.'

'Word on the street says your EA might be looking for

a new job. Or a new husband. Or both. She was wasted on you. The woman needs a real challenge.'

Never.

Over his dead body.

The rage boiled and spilled over. He moved from his chair, the legs scraping back, grabbing his nemesis by the shirt. 'Leave her alone. If I ever hear you've been bothering Simone—'

'Then what? You'll try and destroy me? You've been trying in your own way for as long as you've been in business and yet I'm still here. It's like you want everything I have,' Rocco taunted. 'And why? I'll tell you. You're just a pretty boy, a pretender with no substance. All envy, when the truth is, I've done *nothing* to you.'

'Done nothing? Ask our father what was done to me. Ask him about—' Leo's voice broke on the thought of his mother's name. Rocco didn't deserve to hear it. 'Ask him about his designs. Remind him that he's a thief who stole them.'

'*Our* father?'

Rocco's eyes widened at those words, a look Leo recognised—shock. Leo released Rocco's shirt and pushed him away. Rocco stumbled back.

'Vito Silvestri. My father. Who had an affair with *your* mother while he was still living with mine.'

Now it was Rocco's turn to grab Leo by the shirt, twisting the neck tight. '*Liar.*'

Leo laughed, but it was a mirthless, mocking sound. 'They were in business together. He stole my mother's furniture designs and then left us destitute. Ask him. Take my DNA, I don't care. It'll prove I'm telling the truth, *brother.*'

He wrenched from Rocco's grasp, a few buttons on his shirt tearing off, scattering on the floor. Then Leo threw some money on the bar—too much for the alcohol that had rotted his gut. But he didn't care. Leo needed to go. He turned and stalked into the night. After all these years of believing Rocco Silvestri knew everything, it might be that he was as much a victim of their father's sins as Leo was.

And knowing that didn't make Leo feel any better at all.

Simone sat in the back of the taxi, caught in Milan's notorious traffic. She tapped her fingers restlessly on her handbag, her stomach knotting painfully. Wanting to get to her destination faster, whilst at the same time wanting to ask the driver to turn round and take her back to her hotel. She reached inside her bag and took out a bottle of water, uncapped it and sipped. It didn't help, just churning in her stomach together with the meagre breakfast she'd picked at, leaving her feeling ill. Because today was important. Today was *everything*.

Like an interview for the most important job of her life.

She took a slow breath, looking out the window at the city that had felt more like home in what had only been a few short months, than New York had in years. Because home wasn't about the place, it was about the people you were with. Or in her case, a person.

Leo. Who'd hurt her more than she'd believed any living human could have.

The man she still loved, with all of her heart.

Others might say she was the fool Leo had accused

her of being, given the things he'd said to her. After leaving the Milan office, it's what she'd believed, at first. That she'd been chasing a fantasy cooked up in her own head, and not reality. That he was yet another person who wanted her only for what she could do for him in some material way, rather than wanting her for the woman she was.

Yet she'd come to the belief, slow at first then with a shocking rush, that what Leo had done wasn't because he felt too little.

It's that he felt far too much.

The taxi moved forwards a few feet, stopped. Horns in the distance blared, the energy here still frenetic even though it appeared everything was at a standstill. A lot like her life.

Since leaving the Milan office what seemed like years ago but in what could be measured only in weeks, she'd been busy. First, nursing her crippling heartbreak. She'd flown straight to California to see Holly, to make sure her now heavily pregnant sister was really okay. There, she'd cried on Holly's shoulder as her sister had held her. It was the first time in years Simone had accepted the support of another person without a fight. It was there those old insecurities had roared back—echoes from her parents, from her ex, from every voice that had ever whispered she wasn't worth it.

Leo's own words too—that he didn't want her. She'd believed him. At first.

Until she'd turned to her phone, ready to delete every photograph of their time together and that's when she'd stopped. Took a giant pause, as if the universe had come to a loud and screeching halt and screamed.

Use your eyes and your heart.

She didn't much trust her heart at that moment, but her eyes? She'd scrolled back through her photographs and in her pain and through her tears she *saw*. Lake Garda and then Milan. Their selfie, where he'd smiled. Not the professional smile that could make him millions but one that was deep and warm and true.

And then she began to really *think*. Not about his words, but his actions. How he'd considered what she might enjoy. How he liked surprising her. How he hadn't left her bedside whilst she'd been in hospital. They were all the actions of a person who genuinely cared.

That's when she'd stopped crying and got busy.

The taxi started moving again. Whatever had been holding them up had cleared. She'd be at Leo's Milan home, *their* Milan home, soon. There she'd fight for him, fight for *them*. Simone had come to realise that while she'd spent her whole life believing she wasn't enough, she strongly suspected Leo felt the same. And wasn't that the trap? Two hurt and broken people believing the one they wanted could never want them in return? In the last few weeks she'd discovered so much more about the man Leonardo Zanetti truly was. Especially since she'd called the company accountant and learned what she could about Rome.

Because, whilst the press liked to write about Milan, Rome was where Leo's real story began.

The taxi finally pulled up outside his house, and she paid, her heart beating a frantic rhythm in her chest. Taking out the keys he'd given her and hoping that he hadn't changed the locks. Trying them.

They still fit.

Just like her and Leo, if only he'd recognise it.

Simone made her way quietly through the house finding him on the back terrace. He sat at the table, laptop open. Working on something because he consumed himself, both personally and privately. She relished the view of him against the backdrop of their home's beautiful garden. His broad shoulders—the ones that had carried so many of her burdens and the burdens of others. Those burdens that he'd kept secret because he'd thought what he was doing showed the worst of him, when really, it showed the *best*.

As she eased closer, it was like he *knew*. Leo stiffened and turned.

The moment those vibrant ocean-blue eyes fixed on Simone, twin aches of love and pain crashed over her like a wave onto the shore. Then she caught his expression—surprise and need, before it hardened and he hid behind the veneer he so often presented to the world.

Leo seemed to unfold from the chair, lifting himself up.

It was then she noticed other things. How he wasn't as put together as normal. Stubble on his jaw, like she'd witnessed in the days after her accident. His hair was a little longer than she'd ever seen him with before, and messy. Like he'd run his hands through it too many times. His shirt, usually pressed and perfect, a bit wrinkled.

He looked like he'd just come home from some corporate battle.

Well, she was here to start an emotional war.

'Simone.'

One word, but it was *full* of meaning. A rough sound, like it hurt him to say the syllables. Then he frowned.

'What are you doing here? Have you forgotten something?'

There were so many answers open to her, but she told him the truth.

'I left because you said you were a bad man. That you didn't want me. I came back because I discovered—you're a liar.'

His eyes widened.

'You're not a bad man. Even though you think you are. And I'm here to remind you of that.' She took a step closer. 'Because I know all about Rome.'

Leo hadn't seen her in over a month and, whilst it might have been a cliché, she was like an oasis in the desert. A cool drink to a parched man.

She stood before him, looking more like herself than he'd ever seen. In a beautiful denim dress, no sleeves. Espadrilles that made her look summery, as if she was about to go to the beach or for a stroll by a lake. Embodied with a casual elegance he'd always known lay inside her. It struck him then, how she'd grown without him. Morphed, like a chrysalis turned into a vibrant butterfly. It ached, seeing her. Knowing without a doubt that she'd moved on without him…

And yet, Rome?

'You've heard the story about Rome. I told you myself.'

'You told me the lies you tell yourself. When are you going to see the truth for what it is?'

He didn't understand. He'd laid out the truths of his past. The things he'd done. Whilst he might pretend he was a better man now, the reality was harsh and incontrovertible. He hadn't looked after his mother and he hadn't looked after Simone. He was, in all ways, a selfish man.

A good man wouldn't have entered into an arranged marriage with his executive assistant to secure a business deal, no matter the merits and knowing what he could do for the company in the partnership. A good man would have been there for his mother. Wouldn't have tried to change the woman now standing before him.

She'd fallen and almost died because she was trying to please him. Just like his mother had fallen because she was trying to ensure she earned enough money for him.

He always hurt those he loved the most…

Loved? No. He loved no one. If he did, he wouldn't have done the things he had. Yet why did it feel something inside him had torn in two and was bleeding in torrents?

'*Morzone.*'

It was as if a shock of electricity jolted through him. A name from a past he wished was more distant. Or wished he'd never heard at all.

'I don't know what you're—'

'*Bazzoni, Antonelli, Riccardo…*'

She kept going. The list went on and on. Names of the families he'd helped extort. Families he'd tried to ruin. Each sin he was required to atone for.

'I know about them, Leo. I know about them all.'

It should have been impossible. 'How?'

'Circolo's accountant. It seems you haven't told anyone you'd asked me to leave and since I'm still your wife and EA…'

He hadn't wanted to admit to anyone that he'd pushed her away, most of all himself. He'd been waiting for the inevitable resignation letter when it would have been impossible to deny the rumours currently swirling round, that all wasn't sunny in the Zanetti household.

'All these people, they show the best of you, not the worst,' she said.

Leo shook his head. 'You know nothing.'

She didn't. Repaying debts owed was meaningless. It was the *least* he could do. Giving back money didn't make the taking of it any better. Because he couldn't give them back the time they'd lost, and money didn't heal all wounds—as he well knew.

There were some people who would never recover from what he'd done. The trauma he'd inflicted.

'I know a lot, because I've spoken to some of the families. They've told me how their lives have been changed, even though they never knew who their benefactor was.'

His blood turned icy. He'd buried that part of his life so well by creating a charitable foundation that gave back to the families he'd once helped to ruin. His greatest shame and yet the heart of all he was. He never wanted it revisited. No one was ever meant to find out.

'Did you tell them who I am?'

'No. That's your story to tell, not mine. What I asked, was whether they'd like to say anything to the person who'd helped them.'

She reached into her bag and pulled out a folder with sheaves of paper in it.

'I have these. Letters to the charity. Thanking you for what you've done. How you've saved each of them. Changed their lives for the better. Look.'

She thrust the folder into his face. He shook his head.

He didn't want to look at the words when all he could see was her.

'You think this is the worst of you?' Simone asked, 'The worst was doing nothing. This is the best. It's not who you were once, Leo, but how a person changes that makes the difference. You rose from your earlier life like a phoenix. You became someone better.'

'Money doesn't change anything, it just papers over wounds.'

'Here's the thing. You have all these people believing you're good. You're the only one who thinks you're bad. Have you ever thought that might mean the problem's not with all of us? It's with how you're thinking about yourself.'

'All I ever do is hurt people. These families. My mother. You.'

Simone cocked her head, frowned. He wanted to smooth that troubled crease away. He clenched his fists instead.

'What do you mean, *me*?'

'You fell because of me. Because of my vanity.'

'You wanted to give me a beautiful gift of that pair of shoes and I wanted to accept them, so I did. My fall was an accident. Just like your mother's. Do you think either of us would want you carrying misplaced guilt for ever? These things aren't your burden to bear. When I was in the hospital…' Simone's voice trailed off, Cracked. She took a deep breath, gave a shaky smile.

Would his mother have wanted this for him? She'd worked hard, long hours, to make his life better. But in the end, he didn't know, because he couldn't ask her. As for Simone…

'You stayed by my side in hospital,' she said. 'Looked after me at home. Those weren't the actions of a bad man, but a good one.'

She walked towards him slowly, almost as if she was scared he'd try to get away.

'I love you. Despite everything. I wasn't looking for it. I wasn't expecting it, but it hit me all the same. You care about your staff. You cared about me. Around you, I began to like who I was again. And I hope, that if I love you, then maybe you can love yourself.'

For so long, he'd been dead inside. Rejected by his father. A petty criminal. Believing himself selfish. Vacuous. Good only for his looks and what he could sell. Yet, it was as if an ember had burst to life inside of him, bright and blazing.

Simone, believing in him. Loving him.

Everything seemed suddenly clearer, like a blindfold being torn from his eyes and he could see for the first time. Those moments when all he wanted to do was please her. To make her smile. Now, Leo didn't think about what he'd done, but how those things had made him feel. Like a good man, a man who was worthy. A man who could make Simone happy.

'Do you love me?' she asked. 'Because I think the man who showed me a waterfall on Lake Garda. Who sat by me every night when I was in hospital. Who created a beautiful room for me in his home that showed he knew who I was. The man who didn't want me to fall again… I think that's a man who loves.'

It was as if every part of Simone had been holding its breath and now, she'd allowed herself the briefest of moments to exhale. He hadn't asked her to leave. He was listening and maybe it meant he might also *hear*. She stepped towards him again, reached out her hand tentatively and placed it in the middle of his chest, the muscles firm and solid underneath.

'This is where I feel it, in my heart. Maybe, if you let go of the things your head's telling you, you might feel something in your heart too.'

She'd almost expected him to step back but he didn't. Instead, he leaned into her touch. His chest rose under her hand, then he shut his eyes. The slightest of frowns on his forehead. She didn't know what he was thinking. All she could do was stand there and hope, as the heat of him burned into her palm. Then his lips parted and he let out an exhale, opened his eyes and stared at her. The deep blue of his intense gaze burning like a pilot light, pointed in her direction.

'I have no idea what I'm doing,' he admitted.

She gave a shaky laugh. 'Neither do I. All I know is how it feels. Like I'm too big for my skin. Like I want to burst from myself.'

'The only way it's any better, that it feels like you finally fit, is if you're with the other person,' he said.

'It's too big to hide or run away from.'

'Because it's all-encompassing.' He placed his hand over hers. 'It takes over your life. It takes over your soul.'

Simone was certain in that moment, that he understood. Her eyes stung with tears and she took a breath of relief.

'It's so easy not to listen, when you don't trust yourself,' she said.

'This marriage was a means to an end. It should never have been that way and you deserve something more.'

'And yet in the end, we still chose each other.'

'Why can't I find someone like you?' he asked, with a smile.

'Maybe you can,' she replied.

'Maybe we always knew we were meant for each other.' Leo laughed and wrapped her in his arms. 'I love you, *cuore mio*.'

My heart. Her home.

'So, what now?'

'Our honeymoon was rudely cut short by an accident. I'm thinking we should arrange another. Verona perhaps?' Leo winked.

She answered with a smile. 'Are you being a romantic, Mr Zanetti?'

'Around you, always, Mrs Zanetti.'

'Then how about Lake Garda? That's a place I'd like to get to know better.'

'*Perfetto*,' he said. 'But right now?'

Leo dropped his head and she rose to meet him. Their mouths capturing each other's. The kiss unlike any that had come before it because this one was full of love acknowledged, not suppressed. After a few breathless minutes of searching lips and hands, of recognition and reconnection, Leo eased himself away, though he didn't let her go. His talented mouth curling into a slow and wicked smile. 'I think we should start the honeymoon here, *tesoro*.'

Simone laughed as Leo swung her into his arms.

'It's the perfect place to begin our lives again.'

* * * * *

Were you blown away by Vows to the Boss?
*Then why not explore these other dramatic stories
by Kali Anthony!*

Engaged to London's Wildest Billionaire
Crowned for the King's Secret
Awoken by Revenge
Royal Fiancée Required
Prince She Shouldn't Crave

Available now!

Get up to 4 Free Books!

**We'll send you 2 free books from each series you try
PLUS a free Mystery Gift.**

FREE
Value Over
$25

Both the **Harlequin Presents** and **Harlequin Medical Romance** series
feature exciting stories of passion and drama.